Waters of D
Third tale in the Di
A novell

Historical Note

This story is historical fiction, not history. That is, it is an imagined tale inspired by real events. Please do not confuse the two. However, the expedition of Theodore Roosevelt to the Amazon jungle really happened. Some of the actual events were too far fetched to be used in fiction. If you would like to know more, I recommend two books. The first is a book written by Roosevelt himself: *Through the Brazilian Wilderness,* pub. May 12, 2012. The colonel revealed many details, but also left out a lot. The other book is *The River of Doubt, Theodore Roosevelt's Darkest Journey,* by Candace Millard, pub. Oct. 10, 2006. Millard fills in a lot of what the colonel left out.

The other inspiration for this book had no connection to Roosevelt, but he was a contemporary. His name was Oscar Hartzell, who you probably have never heard of. He was one of the most successful confidence men of the last century. He perfected the "estate con," making millions from his suckers. One of its descendants is the Nigerian Banker scam. You can read about Hartzell on Wikipedia. He came to believe his own con was real, and lost his mind. Or at least he wanted us to think so . . .

I wish to thank Joyce Anderson for her encouragement and valuable suggestions.

Dying

Martino DiPaolo knew he was dying. For several days - weeks - he had known, but had done his best to deny it. Now, this late in the day, he was lucid enough to accept what was. He raised his head from his litter enough to look around at the teeming jungle. The silence continued to amaze him. He had read books and articles about jungles. Always they described the sounds, calls of birds, rustle of leaves, screech of monkeys, native drumming. This Amazon was different. It was uncannily silent, like some vast monster waiting to pounce.

It had already done that - pounced. This expedition was likely doomed, dying though not yet dead. DiPaolo stared at the ceiling of green leaves above his head. Tiago appeared in his field of vision, silent as the forest around him.

"Acordado? Sveglio?" Portuguese and Italian. Awake? he asked. Tiago could manage English fairly well, but he was Brazilian. Early in the expedition he and DiPaolo discovered they could understand each other's Latin languages better than the Saxon. They were learning to communicate in a personal patois of their own. DiPaolo lifted an arm in answer to his question.

"Acqua?"

DiPaolo nodded. Tiago raised DiPaolo's head and lifted a jar of cold water to his lips. DiPaolo drank quickly, nearly gagging. His fever was down for the moment, but he knew it would return. He asked in Italian, "What day is this? What is happening?"

"Don't know what day. We stalled. Rondon goes to look for portage trail. You been out for two, three days. Need food."

DiPaolo tried to smile. "Is there any food left?"

"I got some dry fish and palm tops. I make you broth."

DiPaolo felt no hunger, only thirst. He said, "I try to eat."

Tiago let DiPaolo's head down onto the rolled up blanket that served as a pillow. Then he disappeared from view. DiPaolo had been inside a tent, but found it too hot and airless, so he'd asked to be moved outside. Now his only shelter was a web of mosquito netting. He breathed deeply, trying to cool his lungs. He drifted off into a half doze, then awoke when Tiago returned. Tiago was a *camerada*, a bearer. The cameradas outnumbered the expedition men by two to one. They carried nearly all the equipment and supplies, as well as paddling the canoes. They bore most of the burden and never complained.

Tiago was spooning a steaming broth into DiPaolo's mouth after propping him up. Before night fell, he would transfer from his litter on the ground to a hammock. Away from all the creatures that crawled and crept. DiPaolo recalled the Colonel's remark, that in Africa there are large beasts like lions, tigers and hyenas that want to eat you. In the Amazon there are *tiny* things that want to eat you. Mosquitoes, biting flies, piranha fish.

DiPaolo remembered the letter that had come in San Francisco, the message that had got him into this. DiPaolo had been enjoying a day off, relaxing with his lover Benita Bernardi, in her parlor. Midsummer, and as usual the city was cold and foggy. They had decided to stay in that day, listen to the gramophone, read to each other. The letter came by special delivery. It was from the Colonel, Theodore Roosevelt.

How would you like to join me on a relaxing adventure to the Amazon jungle? I still appreciate your past service to me. I should like to reward you with a rare opportunity to visit one of the few remaining wildernesses. It should be a bully trip, canoeing down a lengthy unexplored river. I plan to bring some of those new fangled light canvas canoes. We plan to be away a month or so. I do hope you can make it ...

The letter was short and to the point. DiPaolo read it twice, then read it again, this time out loud to Benita. He shook his head. "That man gets bored in civilization. I guess he assumes everyone else likes living in tents and shooting elephants for dinner. A crazy idea."

Benita grinned. "No elephants in the Amazon, that I know of. Maybe he'll discover some. You should go."

At that he gaped. "Do you want to get rid of me?"

She giggled. "Just for awhile, so I can enjoy my other six paramours. No, really, Martino. You deserve time off. You take your work too seriously. Getting away for a month will give you some perspective. When you come back I'll love you all the more."

"Come to that, I wonder why this invitation doesn't include you."

She shrugged. "Sounds like a boy's club sort of adventure, traipsing through the jungle, fighting off wild Indians and so on. I don't think I'd much care for it."

He sat down, giving the letter some thought. Reading it for a fourth time. "I'm still searching for Kwanyin Luk. I want to see that man in prison."

"He'll still be there, wherever he is, when you return."

And so it was decided.

IN HIS DELIRIUM, DIPAOLO did not so much remember the next scene as relive it. That had been back in Concepcion, that civilized port city. Colonel Candido da Silva Rondon had been appointed official guide to Roosevelt's party. The two colonels were still getting to know each other. Rondon had been there waiting at Bahia. So had Kermit, Roosevelt's son, who was also in the party. From there they had taken a boat to Concepcion, the lovely capital of Paraguay.

Rondon leaned over a map stretched out on a table, pointing. He said, "We begin here, on the Paraguay side of the border. From there we begin our descent of the Tapajos." He went on to point out the other rivers they planned to visit, all clearly marked. Roosevelt leaned closer, adjusting his spectacles. He was notoriously near-sighted. After studying the map for half a minute he said,

"Those rivers are all mapped."

"So they are, sir."

Roosevelt took off his glasses, rubbed them with a bandanna, put them back on. He smiled, looking directly at Rondon. "I see there are large areas of this map with nothing on it."

"True, sir. Brazil is still largely unmapped."

Roosevelt still smiled. "There is not much scientific value in exploring areas already mapped."

At that Rondon stared back at Roosevelt. For a moment it was as if they read each other's minds. Rondon nodded, said nothing. Roosevelt said, "Bully. Let's do something difficult instead of an easy job." They shook hands. And so the itinerary was changed. They selected a different river to explore, one almost totally unknown. Il Rio de Duvidas. The River of Doubt.

A Strange Letter

When DiPaolo left San Francisco to join the expedition, he put his best man, Jack Harrow, in charge of the DiPaolo detective agency. He also left instructions in writing for him to comply with anything Benita Bernardi might ask. He didn't expect she would need to ask, but that was a normal precaution.

DiPaolo had become something of a celebrity since his involvement with the former President Roosevelt. So a brief note appeared in the Society pages of the *San Francisco Examiner,* headed *DiPaolo to accompany Roosevelt.* Subheading: *Looks forward to exciting expedition.*

Bernardi was looking forward to a few weeks of peace and quiet. With Martino around, there was usually more excitement than she wanted. About a week after his departure a strange letter showed up in the mail. It wasn't special delivery, though it was on expensive stationery. The return address was in London, England. It was addressed to DiPaolo, but he had left instructions for her to handle any business that came up. She opened the letter. It read in part,

Esteemed Mr. DiPaolo,

I am attorney of record working with Sr. J.C.T. Pascual, who is executor for the estate of the Marquis de Paolo. The Marquis passed away intestate some eighty-two years ago. Due to various social upheavals, it was impossible to probate the estate until recently.

In the meantime, the estate in question has been gathering interest and is now believed to be valued at nearly one billion dollars U.S.A.

One of my tasks is to locate and verify all eligible heirs to this estate. My investigations show that you, Mr. DiPaolo, are one of these heirs.

Please respond to this letter as soon as possible. I am requesting any documents you may possess showing your line of familial descent for the last century. If you do not have such documents at once available, I may assist you in obtaining such. My preliminary estimate of your share of the estate would be approximately one million, six hundred thousand dollars after legal fees are deducted.

Looking forward to hearing from you,
I am your obedient servant,
Leon Leatherdale, Atty, Barrister

Benita Bernardi put down the letter, having read it twice. Something smelled wrong about it. That was quite a large sum of money. She could simply file the letter, awaiting Martino's return. But he might not be back for a month or two. If this letter turned out to be legitimate, she wouldn't want to risk him losing. And he had given her an order to handle his affairs while he was gone. Tomorrow she would go down to the DiPaolo Detective Agency. Let them do some detecting.

SEVERAL DAYS LATER Jack Harrow showed up at Bernardi's home, having first telephoned for an appointment. She could have gone to his office, but she supposed he wanted to show respect for his boss's lady. Harrow was in command of the agency while Martino was gone. She made him comfortable in the parlor while he produced his files. He had declined tea or coffee, but took a glass of water. He said,

"We couldn't find anything wrong, at least so far. This Leatherdale is licensed as both attorney and barrister in London. That's unusual. Most men make it a specialty of one or the other. Not like American law, where we don't make any distinction. In England it's different. Lawyers do criminal, barristers civil. At least that's how I understand it.

Anyway, Leatherdale has been doing business for about twenty years. He's legitimate as far as we can tell. This J.C.T. Pascual is another matter.

"He's an Italian. All we know about him is that he's from Naples, but currently living in London. At least we think so. Leatherdale wouldn't tell us his address, citing confidentiality. There really was a Marquis di Paolo. He was in Sardinia, and may have died intestate. Again, it's difficult to get details because of all the upheavals Italy has gone through. Apparently Leatherdale has found other possible heirs to the de Paolo fortune, but I don't yet have a complete list. I can give you a few names, if you want to contact them. Or if you want me to."

She shook her head. "I don't think so. You have done a good job, Johnny. More than I asked for. I'm going to answer Mr. Leatherdale's letter and see what develops. I'll let you know if I need more help."

Harrow grinned, gave her copies of his files, and found his own way out.

That evening she composed a letter.

Mr. Leatherdale,

Mr. DiPaolo is abroad at this time and not expected to return for some weeks. He has authorized me to manage any legal questions in his absence. In reply to your letter of the tenth inst., the only document I can readily locate is Mr. DiPaolo's family Bible. He has managed to retain it since childhood. It is an Italian translation, and the first several pages record a list of family births, deaths, and marriages. I believe most courts would recognize this as a legal document, barring more officially registered certificates. As you know, nearly all civic records in this city were destroyed in the fire of 1906. I do not know what records, if any, Mr. DiPaolo might have had on file here.

I cannot let the above Bible out of my hands in Mr. DiPaolo's absence. However, if you feel it may be of evidential value, I may arrange for a photographic copy of the relevant pages and forward them to you. I regret I may not be of more help at this time.

Sincerely,

B. Bernardi

Next day, she had the letter typed and took it in person to the Post Office. Then she shrugged and went down to the police station to chat with the boys. She wasn't going to worry about a million and some dollars.

Kwanyin

Kwanyin Luk was happy. So far this was proving to be a perfect confidence game, and the most lucrative one he had ever tried. He looked forward to today's interview with the barrister Leatherdale. As usual the manservant let him in to Leatherdale's apartment on Fleet Street.

"And how are we today, Mr. Leatherdale? I hope I find you well?"

Leatherdale looked up from his desk, where he seemed to spend most of his days. He held a French language newspaper in one hand, a large magnifier in the other. He looked up, blinking myopically through his spectacles. "Who is it? Ah, Pascual. I had forgotten our appointment. Yes, thank you, I am well today. I hope you are the same. Will you take tea?"

"I would be pleased to do so." He nodded at the manservant, whose name he had never got quite straight. The man moved off toward the kitchen to fetch tea. "May I sit?"

"Yes, surely. Please do. How goes our project?"

"Slowly, sir, but I am satisfied. There would be no point in trying to rush. I have here a draft for your usual fee. I shall place it on your desk." The amount of the draft was a mere pittance of what Luk was bringing in, but it didn't matter since Leatherdale would probably forget about it anyway. Luk had convinced the lawyer he himself was Italian, though he knew not a word of that language. If Leatherdale had better eyesight, and if his senility were less advanced, he would have seen that Luk was Oriental. Luk of course spoke English with a British accent, having been educated at a missionary school in Hong Kong. He said, "I contemplate a brief visit to the States. It appears that many of the di Paolo heirs I have located are to be found there. I shall of course keep you informed."

"Yes, yes. Ah, the tea, I could use some. How about some biscuits, Charles? Very good. Now, what were you saying?"

Kwanyin Luk opened his briefcase. "I shall be needing your signature on a few documents here. Petitions and letters, the usual routine forms. You needn't bother read them, they're just paperwork."

In fact, Luk had just returned from the States. It was now several weeks since he had first sent that letter to Benita Bernardi. He had been inspired when he saw the notice about DiPaolo going on a safari, or whatever it was supposed to be. He immediately composed that letter to DiPaolo, as well as a number of others. In all, he had sent out about two hundred letters to people found in city directories who appeared to have Italian surnames. Many of them had responded with cash. As had Bernardi.

Not that he believed for a moment that DiPaolo was going off to Brazil with Roosevelt. DiPaolo for some reason wanted to disappear from public view for awhile. Kwanyin suspected his reasons might have something to do with DiPaolo's search for Kwanyin.

"We have known each other a couple of years now, haven't we?" he said to Leatherdale.

"Have we? Time does fly."

"Indeed." This was not the first game Luk had played with Leatherdale. The man made a perfect front with the British court system. Luk had manipulated him to represent, on paper, several lucrative lawsuits and claims which had resulted in ready cash. Usually it wasn't necessary to bring the man to court. When he did, Leatherdale would sit quietly listening or staring around the room while Luk did the talking for him. Luk himself was constantly amazed at the gullibility of even barristers and judges.

He got Leatherdale's signature on several promissory notes. These were receipts for contributions to the legal defense fund. Luk could have forged the signatures, but he wouldn't take the chance. He would have the barrister's manservant sign as witness before leaving London.

A week or so after sending off her response to Leatherdale, Benita Bernardi received a second letter.

Jungle

Tiago and another camarada disappeared into the forest to search for food. They returned hours later with a sackful of Brazil nuts. That would be a welcome protein. Someone else had shot a monkey. DiPaolo at first had been queasy about eating monkey meat. It made him think of cannibals. But when a man is hungry enough, cannibalism becomes an option. He would have eaten every monkey in the jungle if he could.

In the evening Rondon shared out nearly all of what rations were left. They knew what this meant. They might all die tomorrow. There was no point in saving.

DiPaolo said, "I'm not sure I can walk tomorrow."

Tiago gave a shrug. "If not, we carry you in hammock. No worries."

"No, I won't have that. Roosevelt won't let himself be carried. Neither will I. If I can't walk, you leave me. I have a gun."

Tiago's gaze went off somewhere into the forest. He said nothing.

That night DiPaolo took more quinine. He drank more water and felt cooler. Then he slept and dreamed. His dreams were incoherent, jumping from one world to another, between Brazil and San Francisco and other places he had been. He dreamed of Benita. He awoke and remembered getting here, all the times he might have left the jungle and saved himself. Back in Bahia, he should have known. The Colonel had shown him around a sort of botanical museum, part of the university. He had been fascinated with poisonous snakes. In Brazil it seemed there were dozens of them. Roosevelt had paused by one particular cage.

"The black mamba," he said. "The most deadly serpent on Earth. One bite and you die in minutes. But this other snake, harmless to humans, likes to eat black mambas." DiPaolo shuddered, remembering. His memories came back to him out of order, as if some events of a month ago had happened yesterday, and vice versa. He slept, dreamed, awoke and remembered again. There was the time they had come across a river full of piranha. Strangely, some parts of that stream were free of those fish, while other pools were packed with them.

Someone had noticed part of a man's shirt floating above the water. He had found a pole and fished it out. They discovered not only a shirt, but pants and shoes. Probably they had belonged to one of those men who came to the forest searching for rubber trees. Inside the clothing they found a complete human skeleton. The piranha had devoured every morsel of flesh and left the bones behind.

DiPaolo now remembered a thing Roosevelt had said even before they began this journey.

"In Africa," he said, "on safari, you encounter some large beasts that want to eat you. Lions, tigers, wolves, hyenas. In the Amazon we find *tiny* things that want to eat us."

At last, morning came. Men took their time getting ready. They had coffee and what breakfast they could find. Each man packed his own gear. Finally they assembled. Rondon spoke up.

"I will lead the way as usual. The trail is already blazed. You should have no problem following it. You will find some parts hazardous, you will have to climb down, or up. Also a number of places you will get your feet wet. Be careful, the current is swift. President Roosevelt, assisted by Kermit, has insisted on taking the rear. Any injured or lame must allow the able bodied to go first, so as not to slow them down. I wish you all the best of luck. May God assist you."

He paused until someone else spoke a brief prayer. Then he led off the portage.

Second Letter

"**W**hat do you think?" Bernardi asked Harrow. He had been studying the letter for five minutes, even holding it up to the light, and comparing it with the first letter. He put it down. He said,

"Don't know what to think, ma'am. It passed my mind it could be a forgery, not from Leatherdale at all. But I think it's genuine. I've been doing a little extra digging on my own. It appears there really are a number of other possible beneficiaries. I don't know how many, but so far I've run across about fifty. They're all convinced it's real. Most of them won't talk about it much, but they're all investing money. How much, I couldn't say. Leatherdale put out a few adverts several months ago, looking for people with the DiPaolo name. That was back east, so you would not have seen it. Nothing about the estate, just asking for names. I put a couple ads out myself, that's how I found some of the heirs. They all assure me they have great confidence in Leatherdale and his fund. It's almost like a stock offering, invest for an eventual return. But it's a private fund, not registered anywhere. I've never seen anything like it."

"Thank you, Johnny." They were speaking in the offices of the DiPaolo Detective Agency. On impulse she had called to make sure he was in, and then come down. She said, "You're doing more than I asked. I'm glad you did. I wish Martino were here. I have not heard from him in weeks now."

"No? When was that?"

"I received a wire sent from a telegraph station in Brazil. It was somewhere in the forest, on the bank of a river. Martino warned me he might not be able to contact me again for some time, since they were leaving the telegraph line. I didn't realize how long it would be. Frankly, I'm beginning to worry."

Harrow smiled. "Martino can take care of himself. And he's with Roosevelt. I shouldn't worry." He held up the letter. "What do you intend to do about this?"

She shrugged. "There's no harm in risking a few dollars, is there? I will send a hundred and see what happens."

Moving

Time to move. Rondon gave the signal and men began gathering what gear they could carry. They had already abandoned much, now they must leave behind even more. DiPaolo looked with regret at the dugout canoes. He himself had helped to carve them, hacking away with an axe until his hands bled. He remembered with regret those lightweight canvas canoes. They would have been ideal for shooting rapids. But Rondon had decided to leave them behind. Fully loaded with all their gear, they would have swamped.

Earlier, they had traded for some boats with an Indian tribe, but then several were lost, sunk, or wrecked. With full cargo, dugouts rode a few inches above the water. Now they would be moving down river with no boats at all. Later they might need to make more, provided they could find the right kind of trees.

Tiago lifted a sixty pound pack to his own shoulders, as well as a rifle. DiPaolo picked up as much as he could carry, which wasn't much. He felt better having eaten, but the fever kept returning in waves. Tiago kept urging him to drink water. DiPaolo said,

"Do you think we may encounter Indians? That village we saw was not deserted." That had been several days before. The party had suddenly come upon an Indian encampment on the bank of the river. The canoes had pulled into the shore so that Rondon could explore it. He reported there was no one home. Yet some of the fire pits were still warm and smoking. Above some of the huts hung human skulls. Rondon left an axe and several good knives on the ground as gifts, to show they meant no harm. They had seen not one Indian. But they knew the Indians were watching them.

Tiago answered DiPaolo's question. "The Indians will be there, but I hope we may not encounter them. They may let us go in peace, or they may attack, I don't know."

"If they attack, we won't stand a chance. They have poison arrows or blowguns. What is their tribe?"

Tiago shrugged. "I don't know. Maybe Cinta Larga. The 'Large Belts.' We might never see them, though surrounded by them. They are more likely to attack than parlay. Headhunters and cannibals. I hope we shall not see them."

One by one, the men moved off onto the portage trail, hacking their way through with machetes or axes. The expedition members carried as much as the camaradas. In this place all men were truly equal. Finally, the only ones left were Roosevelt and Kermit. Kermit looked at DiPaolo and Tiago. "You go ahead. My father and I will take the rear guard."

"No sir," DiPaolo said. He still saw himself as one of Roosevelt's bodyguards. A protector. "Tiago and I take the rear. You go ahead."

"Suit yourself." Roosevelt, leaning heavily on his son, moved off with him into the bush. He gave one backward glance and nodded. DiPaolo took that as a thanks.

Then Tiago and he were alone. DiPaolo had fashioned a walking stick for himself. He forced himself to move forward onto the trail. For two or three hours then, he and Tiago pushed ahead. Most of the trail had been blazed, so there was not much need for the machete. They followed an embankment alongside the river, which below had become a raging torrent. Huge rocks projected above the current. They would have destroyed any dugout in minutes. At times the trail was low, almost to water level. At others it went inland, away from the water, but they still heard its roar.

Tiago stopped at one curve in the path. He pointed at something. "Look there."

"At what?" DiPaolo wiped sweat from his eyes. He saw nothing but jungle plants, vines, shrubs, trees, every conceivable form of vegetation, all competing for space and sunlight in this jungle hell.

Tiago bent and pointed. "See there? That twig is broken."

DiPaolo leaned over to look. "Yes? So what?"

"Not broken by one of us. That has been there awhile. It's a pointer. It means there is a village that way."

DiPaolo could think of nothing to say to that. He had heard of such "Indian sign," but would never have noticed one.

"How do you know it wasn't just broken by accident?"

Tiago gave a short laugh. "A white man might break it by accident. He wears clothing, shoes, pants, jacket, carries a pack. Lots of things to catch on the branches. The Indians go naked. They break twigs only on purpose. This portage follows an Indian trail, but we can't go through without hacking away with our knives and axes. Too narrow for us, plenty of room for a native."

They pushed ahead. They had fallen behind Roosevelt and his son. DiPaolo wasn't sure how much longer he could go on. The only thing that kept him going was knowing that if he collapsed, Tiago would try to carry him. DiPaolo would not allow that. They stopped once to eat a little food and drink. The plan was for the expedition to meet at the end of the rapids. They would wait for late comers. But they would not wait long. If a man didn't make it out, no one would go back to search.

DiPaolo and Tiago pushed ahead. They stopped when it grew dark.

Pascual?

Jack Harrow read the wire from London. He would have liked to go there himself, but he had not the time or money. Bernardi might have financed the trip, but he would not ask without more evidence. At this point he had little more than his own curiosity. So far he had been lucky to find a contact in a London detective agency. The fact that DiPaolo was known to be a friend of Roosevelt had greatly helped.

The telegram didn't tell him much. The agent had been able to verify the existence of one Juan Pascal, age about seventy. He had been some kind of Italian attorney or civil judge, it wasn't clear. He had emigrated to Britain some years ago. Present whereabouts unknown. The agent promised to keep looking.

Harrow had not discouraged Bernardi from sending that one hundred dollars, though that would be more than a month's wages for many people. He had an instinct about this. Bernardi had taken the bait. Now Harrow wanted to grab hold of the line and haul in the fisherman for a closer look. He glanced up at the portrait of Martino DiPaolo that hung in the reception area of DiPaolo's offices. In Harrow's mind, he talked to DiPaolo.

Well, boss, I hope this turns out to be a real deal. I hope you inherit a million. I just don't want you to come home and learn that your woman has been snookered with your fortune. Then Harrow grinned. He thought, *I bet you're having a grand time in the Amazon. You deserve a long vacation. I guess you'll come back happy and rested.*

KWANYIN LUK ARRIVED in San Francisco. He had not been back for nearly a year, but he had maintained a few contacts in Chinatown. So far he had been careful to avoid a bad reputation there. It was dangerous for him in New York or Hawaii, where he had been caught extorting cash from gambling dens. The tongs had long memories. After settling in to a good Chinese rooming house, he set up a meeting with a man calling himself Daniel O'Shea. They met in a back room of a good restaurant. O'Shea had come recommended by some of Kwanyin's contacts who often worked with connected white criminals.

Kwanyin knew at once O'Shea was not Irish, and that was hardly his real name. By his accent, Kwanyin guessed he might be of Polish parentage. It didn't matter, as long as he could navigate in respectable white business circles. That he could do.

Over dim sum, Kwanyin outlined his current scheme. O'Shea listened in silence, carefully dipping his food in sauce, using chop sticks. Kwanyin was impressed. He thought this was a man who could make himself comfortable in any society. When Kwanyin finished talking, O'Shea sipped his tea. "How much you paying?"

"One thousand up front, then five percent of the monthly take."

O'Shea nodded. "Ten percent. Sounds fair. When do I start?"

"I would prefer tomorrow morning. You can set up an office here. Or you could move back east if you choose. So far most of my clients are in Iowa or other Midwest states, but I'm hoping to bring in more out west. There are a lot of Italians in San Francisco."

"This does sound like a good plan. I handle the correspondence and book keeping. You do the research. You are Pascual, back in London. In case you get caught, I'm only the office boy. Why are you spending so much time in London? Why not stay here?"

At that Kwanyin smiled. "Isn't that obvious? All the marks are here in the States. But I'm not breaking any laws in Britain. They can't touch me there."

O'Shea leaned across the table to shake hands. "I think we have a deal, Mr. Kwanyin."

JACK HARROW GOT OFF the train in Fort Dodge Iowa, checked into a hotel and headed straight for the man he wanted to talk to. Bernardi had agreed to let him have a few days off just for this trip. He had placed a notice in several midwestern newspapers asking for presumptive heirs of the Marquis di Paolo fortune to contact him. He had received three answers. Only one had agreed to an interview. Harrow had to see him in person. The man's name was Costello. He lived with his wife in a small row house. Harrow knew nothing else about him. On meeting him, he guessed the couples were both in their seventies.

"Mr. Costello. It is so kind of you to meet with me."

Costello glanced up and down the street before closing the door, as if checking for spies. "Come on in. The missus has coffee on, you want any."

"No thanks, sir, I'm fine. I just wished a few words with you, if I may."

"Sure, sit down, take a load off. What you want to know?"

"Well sir, first I wanted to thank you for agreeing to see me. I'm just looking for more information about this investment, before I decide to put money into it. I guess you must somehow be related to this Marquis di Paolo?"

Costello grinned, leaning back in his easy chair. "That I am, I got the papers to prove it. I paid a genealogy expert. I guess by this time next year I'll be rolling in dough. I got two kids, boy and girl. They don't live at home anymore, both got married. Be nice to be able to leave them a fortune."

"Yes, indeed. Do you mind, sir, if I ask how much you have invested?"

Costello pushed the suspenders off his shoulders to get more comfortable. He shrugged. "Why not? Two thousand, so far. I might put up more later. I'll be getting back five hundred for every dollar. That comes out to a cool million."

"Yes, it does. Did you send a personal check?"

"No, Mr. Pascual don't take checks. Either cash, bank draft, or postal order. I sent a draft, got the receipt."

That disappointed Harrow. He had hoped to see where a check was cashed, in what bank account. "And how did you first hear about this - investment?" He almost said "scheme."

"Personal letter. It came by Registered. I save all the letters. Want to see them?"

"Yes, I wouldn't mind, if you don't." He tried not to sound eager.

The letters were all professionally typed on expensive bond, with Leatherdale's return address. There were six of them, five signed by Leatherdale, the last by JCT Pascual, signed in an entirely different hand. They were all postmarked in London. He said, "Did you ever meet with Mr. Pascual or Leatherdale in person?"

"Naw. Didn't have to. I know a few others who invested. All smart fellows, educated. One's a dentist. I know if they trust him, I can too. I expect I'll meet the gent when we go to court. I might have to go to England. I've got complete confidence."

Harrow nearly choked on that word, *confidence*. As in *game*. He said, "What sort of work did you say you did, before you retired, sir?"

Costello drew his shoulders back with pride. "Machinest first class. Made pretty good money, too. I might still be working, except I got me a bad back."

"I'm sorry to hear that, sir. I hope you get better." He put the letters down on the end table. "You said you know some others who have invested. Do you suppose I might meet with some?"

"Sure, why not? I'll get on the telephone this evening. You come back and see me, say day after tomorrow. I'll set it up."

"I do appreciate your help, sir. It always pays to be careful when investing."

Costello saw him out. Before Harrow was out the door, Costello leaned close to speak in a low tone. "No, the missus don't believe in our good fortune. She thinks it's too good to be true. Calls me a dumb wop, would you believe it? But let me tell you, put some money into this venture. There's plenty to go around. Mr. Pascual says the estate is worth about a billion by now. You won't regret it."

Bemused, Harrow wondered who might have regrets when this business was done. If it ever was.

Strangers

DiPaolo and Tiago made no fire. It would have been pointless. Fire would be useful for cooking, but they had nothing to cook. They had a few hard biscuits and some Brazil nuts, nothing else. And the night was warm. They strung their hammocks from trees and lay in the dark. Moonlight, if there was any, did not penetrate the dense canopy of forest. Before he fell asleep, DiPaolo hear Tiago reciting a prayer in the Brazilian dialect. DiPaolo tried to listen for sounds, but slept almost at once, exhausted. He did not wake until dawn. Tiago was poking him in the ribs, muttering a single Italian word in a hoarse whisper. *Attento!* "Careful!" And then, *Sonosciuto!* "Strangers!"

DiPaolo awoke with shock, rising to look around. The sun was yet low, the jungle in deep shadow. For a moment he did not see them, then everything came to focus. There were three Indians at the edge of the clearing, spread well apart. Each held a short bow with an arrow knocked.

"Attento," Tiago said again. *Careful.* The Indians wore almost no clothing, other than narrow belts over their privates. They all had various tattoos or body paint, it was hard to tell which. They stood perfectly still, watching Tiago and DiPaolo. DiPaolo could see their eyes darting back and forth, the only movement they betrayed. He thought quickly. He carried no rifle or shotgun, but he had a forty-four caliber Colt revolver. It was in his backpack, which hung on a tree. Tiago had been carrying it along with his own, since DiPaolo was still too weak. Now there was no way to reach it in time.

Tiago spoke a few words in an Indian dialect. It brought no response. Tiago, his empty hands held out, spoke a few more words. This time the Indian in the middle lowered his bow. He spoke a few words in his own language. Tiago turned to DiPaolo. "At least they are not Cinta Larga. I don't know what tribe they are. Their language is a bit like one of the dialects I know. I mean, I understand a few words in it. I don't know if they have ever seen white men."

The Indian who had lowered his bow was gesturing with one hand. DiPaolo said, "What do they want?"

"They want us to go with them. I don't think we should argue."

"Our backpacks ..."

"No. Leave them. Maybe we can come back later. They might leave them alone. If we brought them they would probably steal everything."

DiPaolo felt a wave of faintness. He still had a vial of quinine pills in his pocket. He swallowed one dry and got to his feet. Then they followed the Indian who seemed in charge into the forest. The two other archers went behind, blocking their retreat. They walked for a long time, DiPaolo had no idea how long. He became desperately thirsty, but they had not even their canteens. He had a feeling that if he were to fall the Indians might choose to kill him. He forced himself to keep moving. Some time later, they burst into a clearing and found themselves in a village. Dawn was breaking.

DiPaolo looked around and gave a low whistle. "I never would have guessed this was here."

"Many huts," Tiago agreed. "Probably not more than two kilometers from the river."

"There's a stream over there, probably a tributary." Already natives were gathering to stare at them. Some naked children came close, pointing and giggling. DiPaolo could see men and women gathered around some small fires, perhaps cooking or eating. It took him a moment to realize what really unsettled him. It wasn't the large town, unsuspected here in the jungle, the number of huts or humans. It was the almost utter silence. None of the Indians made any noise. Many of them moved closer to stare, sometimes point or gesture. None of them shouted or spoke more than a whisper. If this had been a town anywhere in the States, with a couple of strange Indians showing up out of nowhere, people would have yelled, whistled, rung bells, possibly thrown things. Here, DiPaolo could have passed by a few feet into the jungle and never suspected this place existed.

They were being prodded forward at the point of arrows. The Indian who had spoken led them toward the center of the village. The huts were all round domes, with a single entrance and a smoke hole, constructed of wood and leaves. DiPaolo guessed there were at least two hundred of them. So probably a population close to a thousand. The Indians pushed them into a large hut near the center. Here they sat on the dirt floor. There was nothing else inside. One of the men remained outside, obviously a guard. After several minutes the leader returned. He put something on the floor, spoke one word, and left again.

Tiago examined the bundle. It was a large basket covered with some kind of woven cloth. Tiago removed the cloth to reveal a jar of water and some pieces of dried fish. He said, "This is good. They do not mean to kill us at once." He handed the jar to DiPaolo, who took a swallow, his throat dry as dust. He handed it back. "This is ceramic. In fact it's a nice piece of pottery. I wonder where it came from."

Tiago examined the jar. "Black and white design. I have not seen this style before." He drank some water and handed DiPaolo a piece of fish. "Better eat while you can."

"This could be poisoned. Or drugged."

Tiago smiled. "If so, we won't be any worse off than we already are."

DiPaolo took another quinine, ate some fish and a few sips of water. He didn't want to guess when they would get more. After that, not much happened. A few boys and girls came to stare through the entrance at them, but were chased away by the guard. DiPaolo, exhausted, lay on the dirt floor and tried to sleep. The day passed in silence. Night fell with utter darkness. They could glimpse the flicker of a few fires in the village, but their hut had no fuel in the fire pit. At some point DiPaolo, awakening, heard the far-off lilting tones of a reed flute. It played its strange song three times through and fell silent. Perhaps a young brave was a-courting.

Late next morning a different Indian entered the hut. He did not announce himself, but simply entered and sat upon the floor, regarding them. He was an older man, with many tattoos and a feathered head dress. He wore several metal bracelets on each arm. It took DiPaolo a moment to realize some of them were gold. Otherwise, he was as naked as all the others. After studying them for several minutes, he spoke a few words. At that, Tiago sat up straight. He replied in an Indian dialect.

Glancing at DiPaolo, he said, "He speaks Nhambiquara. Not his language, nor mine, but I can manage it. He wants to know what we're doing here."

"What will you tell him?"

"The truth. We're just passing through." He turned back to the Indian and spoke slowly in that strange tongue. When he finished, the Indian nodded. He seemed to think a moment, then spoke again. It struck DiPaolo strange to use the Nhambiquara as a common tongue. That tribe was one that Colonel Rondon had only recently made friendly contact with. They were still headhunters and cannibals. DiPaolo wondered how Tiago had come to speak it.

The Indian spoke a few sentences or phrases. Tiago nodded and said something in reply. Then the Indian simply arose and left the hut. Tiago said, "I didn't quite get his name. It means something like Teller of Tales. He didn't ask for ours." Tiago fell silent, staring at the hut wall.

"What else did he say?"

"Oh. Just that we cannot leave. He will see us again when he consults with the chief. I told him you are sick with fever."

Two or three hours later another Indian entered. This was an older woman, as naked as everyone else here. DiPaolo still could not get comfortable with all the nudity, and often blushed. This woman had another basket of food. She also had a packet of dried herbs folded in leaves. She gave this to DiPalo and made signs that he should chew them. DiPaolo glanced at Tiago, questioning.

"I think it's medicine. Take it, it probably won't kill you."

DiPaolo shrugged. Nothing to lose. He put the herbs in his mouth and chewed. They had a bitter taste and flooded his mouth with saliva. He swallowed to keep from choking. Almost at once he had a dizzy spell, but then it stopped and he sensed a chill. That was better than the fever. It was some time before he could eat. When he did, he found in the basket not dried fish, but some kind of starchy root. It had a sweet and pleasant taste. For the first time in weeks he felt like eating.

The next day, three Indians they had not seen before dragged them out of the hut. They marched forth from the village.

The Con

J ack Harrow was surprised at how much he was learning about the con, once he got started in Iowa. By now he was convinced it was a con, though he couldn't yet prove it. Mr.Costello had given him the names of two of his friends who had invested. Harrow went to see them, and they were eager to give him more leads. Apparently no one was trying to keep secrets.

He interviewed one "investor" who turned out to be a middle aged widow who had inherited her husband's farm. She herself lived in town and paid someone to manage the property. Judging by her home, she was doing well. Her name was Greta Dunning.

"No, I'm not Italian," she said. "Dunning is my maiden name, I go by that now. My dear husband's name was Domingo Garifolo. I'm not sure exactly how he was related to the marquis, but Mr. Pascual assures me the genealogy shows him a descendant, and therefore an heir. Yes, I certainly look forward to getting this legal business settled once and for all. I have invested two thousand, so far. It costs a pretty penny, don't you know, to pursue legal action at the chancery court in England. Oh, but you should invest something yourself, while you still can. You need not be an heir. You can now purchase a share of the enterprise, for as little as twenty-five dollars. That will go to defray legal expenses. And you will have a guaranteed return of five hundred for each dollar. That comes to—"

"Twelve thousand, five hundred dollars," Harrow finished. His head was beginning to spin.

As it turned out, there were other prospective heirs to interview, in various parts of Iowa. Everyone he met knew one or two others and readily gave up their names. No one tried to keep it secret. Harrow now presented himself as a reporter for the *San Francisco Examiner,* working on a major story about this investment opportunity. One of them was a young high school mathematics teacher named Swenson. He said, "No, I'm not in line to inherit, more's the pity. Not a trace of dago in my line. However, I have purchased several shares at twenty-five bucks each. Here, I'll show you." He pulled one from a desk drawer and handed it over. It was a beautifully engraved certificate printed with green ink on good stock. Swenson said, "I keep the others in my safe deposit box. I just keep this one around to show folks if they're interested. Now, of course I investigated before investing. I checked out the facts, looked up the Marquis di Paolo and the court case. I wrote to London and verified the credentials of this Leatherdale. He confirmed there's a pending court case in chancery. It's all on the up and up. That case will be coming up any day, and we're going to get rich." Swenson beamed.

"I see. And you paid for all these shares with bank drafts or postal orders?"

"Yes, of course, that's most secure. Well, all except the first one. I was new to the game and didn't know better. But Leatherdale accepted my personal check anyway, though he cautioned me to be more careful in the future."

"Interesting." Harrow rubbed his chin. "Do you still have the canceled check?"

"Of course. I'm always careful about records and such." He returned to the desk, rummaged a moment, and held out a slip of paper. Harrow looked at the back. It was endorsed by *J. Pascual* but deposited to a bank in New York City.

"I thought Mr. Pascual was in London."

"Oh, he is, but he has an account in New York. That makes it much easier to transfer funds, instead of having always to convert to pounds sterling and so on. In fact Mr. Pascual has just opened a PO box in New York. All donations go to that address, then they go right to the bank."

"Of course." There was an account number below the endorsement. Harrow made a note of the bank and number. "Thank you, Mr. Swenson. You have been a great help. No doubt I'll soon be investing for myself."

Swenson grinned. "Just make sure you don't wait too long and miss out."

Harrow interviewed several other potential heirs and investors. They all had similar stories to tell. All of them had highly professional correspondence in their files, signed either by Leatherdale or by the executor J.T. Pascual. Some of them had detailed genealogy reports showing them descended from the Marquis di Paolo. After a week of snooping Harrow sent a wire to Benita Bernardi. *Don't send more money. It's a con.* He made up his mind to get Bernardi's hundred dollars back.

He would start with the bank.

HARROW ARRIVED AT GRAND Central in New York early on a Monday morning. He had wired Bernardi he'd be taking more time off, as unpaid leave. It was up to her if she later chose to reimburse him for expenses. Harrow had caught a scent and meant to follow it. He could nearly smell the blood.

In new York he looked up an old acquaintance, a scratch he knew only as Jimmy. Harrow's own past was not squeaky clean. He had come to the DiPaolo Detective Agency by way of a two year stint with the Burns agency. Before that, he'd worked as a beat cop in New York. That was one reason he'd decided to move west. He had been getting to know the underworld better than he wanted to. Some of the other coppers had it in for him because he wouldn't take bribes. He didn't take bribes from Jimmy the scratch even though they were offered. Nor did he try to arrest him, because Harrow knew Jimmy had certain people in his pocket. He did get to know him well, and they became, more or less, good friends.

A *scratch* was the term used to describe Jimmy's profession. In underworld slang it meant a forger. Jimmy could give you any kind of document you cared to pay for, from a thousand dollar bill to a fake passport. Harrow had no problem looking him up. He went to a certain saloon on the Lower East Side and asked around if anyone had seen Jimmy the Scratch. No one knew him. No one had seen him. Nobody there had ever heard of anyone by that name. Harrow asked around at a couple other saloons with the same result. Then he walked over to Greenwish Village, found an empty bench, sat down and unfolded a newspaper. He was just getting in to the sports pages when Jimmy appeared.

"How you doin', Jack?"

Harrow folded his paper. "Isn't this a coincidence? I was just thinking about you, Jimmy. Sit down a spell and tell me how you've been."

Jimmy glanced around with his usual caution, sat down and lit a brown cigarette. "I heard you moved out west."

"So I did, Jimmy. I got me a good detective job in Frisco. Also a few jobs on the side. You think you might do a favor for an old friend?"

"What you need, Jack?"

So Harrow described what he would need. Jimmy said, "I'll want a little time to do that right. Say, three days. It's gonna cost you fifty."

"Not a problem, Jimmy. Ten now, the rest when you're done." He passed over a bill.

Jimmy wrote something on a scrap of paper and handed it over. "I'm here on East Third for awhile. You come on over tomorrow morning, say about ten. Bring your documents."

"Thanks, Jimmy. I'll owe you one."

Jimmy tossed away his cigarette. "You'll owe me forty bucks." And he was gone.

Harrow waited a few minutes before leaving. He finished reading the sports. He folded the paper and laughed silently to himself. This was going to be fun.

A WEEK LATER HARROW made his move. He had taken the time to acquire a fancy business suit at a used clothing store. He'd also bought a brand new silk shirt and tie. A fake diamond stick pin and fancy pocket watch completed the outfit. The watch was from a pawn shop and didn't work, but that didn't matter. It was meant for show.

He showed up at the downtown office of the Bank of New York shortly after opening time. That was where Swenson's canceled check had come from. Harrow asked to see one of the bank officers and was duly brought to the proper desk. He handed over his documents. He said, "My name is Jason Pennfield. Here is my personal identification, a United States passport and documents to verify I am licensed to practice law in the state of New York."

The officer glanced over these papers. He'd introduced himself as Mr. Andrew Schmidt. He had the corpulent look of too many years at a desk job, and a bored expression not usually seen so early in the morning. He said, "And what may we do for you today, Mr. Pennfield?"

Harrow presented another set of documents. "As you can see, these authorize me to establish a joint account with Mr. J.T. Pascual, who has an account here. This is the account number. All duly signed, witnessed and notarized."

"I see." Schmidt studied the documents, then got to his feet. "I'll just be a moment." He went off to some back office, where Harrow assumed he was checking on the Pascual account. He returned with a thick file. He said, "The signatures match. I understand why Mr. Pascual would want a joint account. He is located in London. It's not convenient for him to appear in person here."

"Of course. Your statements will show a good deal of cash flow here, both in and out. Mr. Pascual needs an American representative in case of some emergency. Else he would have to rely on American Express."

Schmidt gave a thin smile. "I see no obstacle here. Please sign this agreement, after reading."

Harrow scanned the paper, accepted Schmidt's gold fountain pen, and signed *J. Pennfield* with a flourish. After some more paperwork, Harrow was provided with a passbook and some temporary checks, as well as the latest monthly account statement. Harrow grinned as he left the bank. He must send Jimmy the Scratch a nice bonus. He'd earned it.

That afternoon, he enjoyed a steak dinner at The Blue Ribbon, a German restaurant on West 44th Street. He had not indulged himself like this in months, or maybe years. Not since he was a New York copper who didn't take bribes, but sometimes enjoyed a free meal when offered. He looked through Pascual's bank statement. The outstanding balance as of this morning was three hundred thousand forty-nine dollars and ninety seven cents. There were a number of recent withdrawals and deposits, both by paper draft and wire. Harrow gave a low whistle. Well, he didn't want to bankrupt this poor Mr. J.T. Pascual, whoever he might be.

After dinner Harrow went down to the American Express office. Using one of the Bank of New York's temporary checks, he sent a wired deposit to the account of the DiPaolo Detective Agency in the amount of two hundred thousand dollars. Then he sent a telegram to Bernardi. "Just deposited your full refund with interest to DiPaolo Agency." Bernardi had full access to that account. The wire continued, "Please withdraw entire amount to your own account at once. Harrow."

Pascual's income and outgo were moving through several layers of accounts. Now it had moved through a new one, as yet unknown to

Pascual. By the time he learned about it Jason Pennfield would have disappeared. So would Pascual's money. Or Kwanyin's.

Entrance

As they left the village they were greeted by the older Indian, Teller of Tales. He carried both their backpacks with no apparent strain. They each would weigh around fifty pounds. He handed them to Tiago and spoke a few words. Tiago translated. "He just said, we should take these. He doesn't want them." Tiago opened his own pack, withdrew a good knife in its scabbard. He handed it back to the Indian. A gift. The Indian accepted it with no comment. Then they were pushed on their way by the three men behind them.

There followed another two or three hour trek through dense forest. DiPaolo's clothing kept getting caught on branches, and his boots were about worn through. The sole of his right boot flapped open, allowing dirt to enter. He was getting blisters. He and Tiago literally crashed through the jungle. The men guiding them made no sound, disturbed not one plant. One man led, the other two followed behind. They did not carry bows or spears, but each had a solid looking war club hanging from a belt.

Suddenly the man leading came to a halt, holding up a hand to signal stop. DiPaolo nearly bumped into him. The leader drew his war club. DiPaolo froze, waiting. There was the sound of a snarl, a rustle in leaves, and a jaguar appeared directly ahead, rushing on the Indian. It happened so quickly DiPaolo barely registered. The jaguar was nearly upon the man, but his club flashed as quickly as the animal's pounce. It connected with bone. The jaguar screamed once, turned and disappeared into the jungle. The leader put down his club and signaled to continue.

DiPaolo's mouth was dry as sand. He had been told the jaguar was the only large animal in this country that would attack humans. He had never imagined he would witness such an event, nor its outcome. He glanced at Tiago, who for once looked as pale as himself. The Indians seemed to shrug off the attack. They moved ahead. DiPaolo wished he had some water.

About an hour later they arrived at the Entrance.

"What is this place?" DiPaolo asked.

Tiago said, "I have never seen anything like this. But I have heard stories."

They had halted in the shadow of a great stone trilithon, two square pillars surmounted by a stone cross beam. DiPaolo guessed the beam would way several tons. He wondered who had put it there, and how. The leading Indian emitted a shrill, trilling whistle. Then he waited. No one moved.

DiPaolo was beginning to wonder if anything would happen, when a group of three men and a woman appeared from behind a screen of leaves. The woman might have been about forty. One of the men was older. The two others were obviously warriors. The old man spoke in a rapid jargon to the Indians with their prisoners. Then he looked at Tiago and DiPaolo. He said, in clear Brazilian, "You will come with us." They turned and went back the way they had come. The two prisoners and guards followed. The dense screen of leaves parted, to reveal a patch of clear sky. What lay beyond made DiPaolo gasp. He halted in his tracks. Tiago said, "I have heard of this. I never thought to see it." One of the guards shoved DiPaolo forward. DiPaolo said,

"What do you call this?"

Tiago said, "Isn't that obvious? It's the lost city."

It was like stepping from one world into another. The jungle stopped at the Entrance. The procession walked into a city street teeming with people. They were mostly naked, though some men and women wore decorative feathers, belts and capes. Children ran wild, screaming or stopping to stare at the two prisoners. In one small plaza some boys seemed to be playing a game with a rubber ball. The buildings were all of stone, some only one story, others up to five. DiPaolo guessed they walked a quarter of a mile. He observed to Tiago, "This city isn't nearly as noisy as San Francisco or other towns. No engines, whistles, or horse's hooves. I guess we're far enough from the river so they never hear it there."

Ahead lay a broad avenue leading to a tall pyramid. Here they turned into a doorway, enclosed by a huge woven mat instead of a door. Light inside came from high windows.

The older Indian spoke a few words to the others. All but the woman and one of the warriors departed. The leader turned to Tiago and DiPaolo and spoke. He said, "My name is Kerkan. Sit on the floor. You will have food and water." He turned and gave some direction to the woman, who went out.

"I am Tiago. How is it you speak my language?"

DiPaolo, exhausted, sank to the floor, which was covered with another mat. Tiago joined him after a moment. Kerkan said, "I was at one of your telegraph stations. Two years I work there. I go to spy and to learn. There were some who wanted to kill you all. I counseled against this. I saw only a few white men, but there are more. It is better to hide from them. They bring sickness and bad things."

Tiago said, "I think you are right about that. Why do you bring us here?"

"We want to know why you follow the river. Why are white men here? They have never bothered us before."

"We only travel through, great Kerkan. We wish to know how the river flows, where it travels."

At that Kerkan gave a blank stare. He said, "I must speak with the chiefs. They will decide. Here is your food. Rest and do not go out."

The older woman returned carrying a basket. It contained a jug of water, cooked manioc, and several other edible items including beans.

DiPaolo drank water and found himself hungry. That was good, it meant the fever was going. Kerkan and the woman left the room, leaving a watchman outside the door.

DiPaolo asked, "Why has no one ever found this city?"

"It does not wish to be found. The forest protects it. If we escape, we lose our way in the jungle and die. There is no path. Did you notice the trees that grow in every street here? They provide a canopy of leaves, with only a few places of clear sky. If one of those new aeroplanes flies over, it will see nothing but trees. I have heard stories of Indians who have been here and come out again. I did not believe."

DiPaolo ate and fell silent, as did Tiago. Light from the windows was fading. Night was falling, though they could not see the sun beyond all the trees. DiPaolo felt better with some food in his stomach. The expedition had been on less than half rations for many days. He said, "When we get back, if we do, will anyone believe us?"

Tiago laughed. "No. I won't even try to tell them. Right now I worry only about getting back."

From outside somewhere there came a blood curdling screech, like a woman being tortured. A howler monkey. Somehow it came as a pleasant sound, a familiar one in a strange world. DiPaolo could remember falling asleep to those distant cries. They were part of the world he knew. He felt a little sorry about having eaten one of those monkeys.

DiPaolo said, "I wonder what happened to Julio?"

"That killer?" Tiago shrugged. "Who cares? No doubt he did not live long."

Julio was the only camarada in the party who could not be trusted. The bad apple. He was caught stealing food. Julio seized a rifle and shot the man who discovered him, then ran into the jungle. Later he'd returned and begged to be taken prisoner, rather than left behind in the Amazon. He was refused, since the party by then had not enough resources to feed and guard a prisoner. So he was left behind.

DiPaolo said, "Roosevelt wanted to shoot him. Rondon would have taken him back to face trial. I guess he got the death sentence anyway."

Tiago turned to look at DiPaolo. "We are not Julio."

Before darkness fell they found the canvas hammocks in their backpacks and managed to string them up by support posts in the room. It was better not to sleep on the hard ground, where all manner of insects might be found. DiPaolo would have liked a light but they had no candles, nor anything to burn. He wished for a lantern and a book to read. Instead he lay down and fell into troubled sleep.

Conners Conned

The man calling himself Daniel O'Shea put down his log book with satisfaction. It was the list of several bank accounts he was managing, in several parts of the country. The receipts were excellent. "Donations" were coming in every day, five dollars here, a hundred there, sometimes as much as a thousand. Mostly from Iowa, but more now from California and other states. Kwanyin had been sending out more award letters every day. And now there were several other agents.

O'Shea found a cigar in his desk, leaned back and smoked. Later he would drop into a fashionable saloon and have a few drinks. He was known there as Danny. Everybody knew Danny and a few knew him well enough to cadge drinks. Now and then he might go and visit one of the upstairs ladies, where he was always generous. Danny was in his element.

So far this was a good con. Kwanyin Luk had put him on to something rich. He would take his ten per cent and probably not try to skim any more. Or not much more. Why queer the deal? Danny knew the difference between a long con and a short one. In a short con, you sold somebody a gold brick and never saw him again. In a long con, you got him to pay installments, maybe for months or years. This Marquis di Paolo scheme could be a great long con.

He picked up the latest wire that had come in about an hour ago. It was a confirmation for a wire transfer in New York. He shook his head. He didn't recall one of those recently. Maybe Kwanyin had done it. He read the wire. Then he put down the cigar and choked. Two hundred thousand transferred to an account in San Francisco. One he had never heard of.

He picked up the phone and called Western Union. He needed to ask Kwanyin about this.

IT TOOK SEVERAL HOURS for the telegram to get through trans-Atlantic traffic to the apartment of Kwanyin Luk in London. By then it was the middle of the night. It was the policy there of the local cable office not to deliver messages at night unless marked as emergency. So it was not until after nine a.m. that a messenger knocked at Kwanyin's door. Kwanyin's personal valet answered, took the message and tipped the delivery man. The valet knocked at Kwanyin's bedroom door. Kwanyin had just finished dressing. "Yes, what is it, James?"

James cleared his throat. "A wire for you, sir. Shall you breakfast out this morning, or should I order the service?"

Kwanyin came out of his bedroom. "What wire? Let me see. Why wasn't it sent to my office?" He ripped open the message, read it twice, then stuffed it into a pocket. "I shall be out today. Any calls, take a message." And he was out the door. James had never before seen him in a hurry. When sure he was gone, James picked up the telephone and dialed room service. "Breakfast for one, please. Room nine eleven." For once James would enjoy a quiet breakfast by himself. Billed to his employer.

Kwanyin took a cab to his London office, which was actually the office of his friend Leatherdale. It was a perfect front. Any money that arrived from the States went directly to a Leatherdale account which Kwanyin had access to. From there he could withdraw funds in the form of cash and deposit to a personal account of his own. The money was untraceable. Of course he also kept large sums in the American accounts. That was where his marks sent their money orders. He needed to keep some capital there to pay expenses, such as advertising and paying hired agents like O'Shea. He had recently hired three more agents in different parts of the country. These were men who actually believed the Marquis story. They all thought they were getting rich. Let them think so, as long as they kept collecting and sending in their donations. He let them keep one per cent each.

He looked again at this wire from O'Shea. Two hundred thousand transfered to an account he'd never heard of. O'Shea had been smart enough to include the account number in his telegram. Kwanyin quickly got off a wire of his own to the New York bank. He demanded to know the name on that account. After that he waited. He thought about breakfast, but instead had coffee. Several cups. By that afternoon he began to get hungry. Then a response arrived from New York. He looked at the name on the account and lost his appetite.

DiPaolo was supposedly out of the country, enjoying himself in some tropical paradise. How had he managed to steal Kwanyin's money? More imporant, how was Kwanyin to get it back? Kwanyin did something that he rarely indulged in. He had a shot of whiskey.

BENITA BERNARDI LOOKED over her own bank book. Jack Harrow had told her to take the money, so she had done so. Now she was having second thoughts. She had trusted Jack to run the detective agency in DiPaolo's absence. Now that he was on leave she had been running it herself, spending several hours a day at the office. The men didn't seem to resent her, but she would have preferred doing something else, something perhaps more fun. Like hanging out at the police station, watching the coppers bring in evil doers. Now she wondered what Jack Harrow was up to.

Two hundred thousand was a serious amount of money. She had drawn a bank draft from the Agency account and taken it personally to her own bank. There would be no canceled check to trace the cash. Harrow's telegram just said it was from Kwanyin's account. It promised a follow-up letter to explain. So she would have to wait a day or two for more information. She lit one of the cigars she sometimes enjoyed and stared out the window. For once the weather in San Francisco was bright and sunny. The view was lovely. She could see the reclaimed land from here, where the city was already preparing for the grand international exposition next year. It would celebrate the opening of the Panama Canal, due to happen this summer. No doubt Roosevelt would be there. As cheerful as ever, despite surviving an assassination attempt and losing an election. The event would really be a proud display of the city's recovery from the disaster of nine years before, the great fire that some claimed would kill the city forever.

Benita stubbed out her cigar, beginning to feel some resentment. Martino DiPaolo was off enjoying himself in some jungle wonderland, leaving her alone to manage this mess and deal with Kwanyin Luk. They hadn't heard from that one for over a year. Of course he had picked this time to crawl from the woodwork. Benita was going to have words with Martino when he got back from his vacation. She hoped he was enjoying himself.

The Chiefs

They awoke when first light filtered through windows. Outside, they could hear sounds of the city stirring, coming to life. DiPaolo, as always, wondered at the great silence that usually hung over this jungle. Other than the sometimes distant screams of howler monkeys, an uneasy quiet prevailed. There were birds, but few bird sounds. No crickets, coyote howls, or frog croaks. It was as if every creature in this forest kept silent hoping not to be noticed by larger, hungry beasts.

Tiago said, "That man said he is not a chief. But his name is Kerkan. Kan means a chief, or a king, or a god. Like Huru Kan in Mayan, what you call hurricane."

DiPaolo splashed water onto a bandanna to wash his face. "I didn't know that. Kan sounds like king in English. Or Khan in Mongolia. I wonder where the word comes from?"

Tiago shrugged. "There's some manioc left over. Better eat some, we don't know when we will again."

"Or if." DiPaolo grinned. His fever had left him in the night.

Kerkan entered an hour or two later. It was hard to judge time without seeing the sun. DiPaolo missed his watch. It was one of the items of equipment he had abandoned to lighten his load. It might not have survived the river anyway.

Kerkan pushed aside the mat and entered without announcement. He looked them over as they rose from the floor. "Come and meet the chiefs," he said.

So without comment they rose and followed him out. Two warriors walked behind. Kerkan led them in the direction of the pyramid. DiPaolo could not guess how high it was without some scale of comparison. It was not like the Mayan or Aztec pyramids, no stairways on the side or temple at the top. DiPaolo hoped this meant it wasn't used for human sacrifice. People were in the streets going about various tasks without much noise. Some stopped to stare at them, especially children. Most chose to ignore them. The adults did not chatter among themselves. It was as if they emulated the creatures of the forest in their silence. Some of the children giggled.

Kerkan led them to a high platform near the pyramid. It stood in the center of a courtyard of its own. This structure had a stairway. Kerkan stopped and pointed, meaning for them to ascend. DiPaolo asked in low tones, "Are they going to cut out our hearts?" There was no reply. At the top of the platform they found five men and four women seated on mats. All of them were heavily decorated with feathers, brightly colored blankets, beads, and other trinkets. DiPaolo could not guess their ages, but none of them were young. Around the perimeter stood several younger men, perhaps warriors. Either guards or witnesses.

Kerkan stood before them and addressed those seated in a few words. He gestured toward DiPaolo and Tiago. Turning, he said in Portuguese, "These are the chiefs of our city. They will question you."

A man seated at the center of the row asked something. Kerkan responded, giving the prisoner's names. His pronunciation in the other language carried a lilting tone. The chief asked another question. His own tone was flat, decisive, demanding. Once again Kerkan answered. He turned back to the prisoners. "The chief has asked what you are doing in this country. I told him the answer you said yesterday. Do you want to say more?"

DiPaolo cleared his throat and spoke up. "Tell your chief we are grateful for your kind treatment. We are strangers in a strange land. We mean no harm and come in peace. We admire your city. We would like to trade if we might. We have many things—"

Kerkan cut him off, turned back to the chief to translate. The chief turned and spoke to those seated next to him. There was a murmur of discussion among the group. Then he spoke again to Kerkan. Kerkan said, "The chiefs have no interest in trade. You have nothing we need or want. Your people carry disease and you disturb the forest. Why do you want to see where the river flows?"

This time Tiago spoke. He said, "Great Kerkan. I am not of the same people. I work for them but do not belong. My grandfather was Indian like yourself, but another tribe. These people treat me fairly and I do not complain. They want to know the river because they are not all in one place. They have many cities, some far apart. You know this because you have been to the telegraph station. They send messages through wires a long way. They travel a long way on rivers. To do that they must see where the rivers go. That is the only reason they are here."

Kerkan seemed to think over this answer for a moment before turning to translate for the chiefs. That group again murmured among themselves. Then one of the women spoke. DiPaolo had heard that some Indian tribes had woman chiefs, but he had never seen one. This lady sat up straight-backed, legs folded under, and spoke in a clear and resonant voice. She was addressing not Kerkan but the other chiefs. Some of them nodded and seemed to agree. Then one of the men at the end of the line spoke up. He sounded angry. There was more discussion among the group. Finally, a decision seemed to be reached. The man who had questioned Kerkan raised a hand and spoke. Kerkan turned back to the two prisoners. He said,

"There is disagreement. A few chiefs think you should be put to death at once. We do not want your people to learn of our city. The woman says we might wait, since you can not leave without a guide. There should not be a quick judgment. In the meantime you will be put to work in our gardens. The chiefs will take time to decide what must be done."

DiPaolo looked at Tiago. Tiago remained without expression. DiPaolo decided it would be best to say nothing. He felt like shouting either in anger or fear. Instead he clamped his mouth shut. As Kerkan led them back to their room, DiPaolo had a chance to cool off. He asked Kerkan, "Does your city have a name?"

Kerkan answered without looking back. He spoke a word in his language which DiPaolo wouldn't have been able to pronounce. Then he said, "That is a name that other tribes call our city. We do not have a name of our own for it. The name they use means in your language, City of Gold."

London

It took Harrow six days to cross the Atlantic. Bernardi had granted him an expense account, but not a lush one. He did not take the fastest liner on the sea. By the time he got to London he decided he hated to travel, especially by water. It took him a day or two to get over being sick. He checked into a cheap hotel room that at least had a bathroom. Next morning, feeling well enough to keep down breakfast, he went in search of the office of Leon Leatherdale, Solicitor and Barrister. Harrow had the bad luck to be picked up by an East Ender taxi driver. Neither could understand the other's version of English. However, Harrow managed somehow to find the correct address.

He spent some time loitering in the street and watching the entrance. For awhile he stood in a phone booth across the street, until someone approached wanting to use it. Harrow strolled to the end of the block and back again. He dawdled in a nearby book store. No one entered or left the place he was watching. After more than three hours on the street a policeman began eyeing him with suspicion. Harrow tipped his hat, smiled, and entered the building. It was a modest four story brick structure, probably early Edwardian. Of course no elevator. Narrow decorative windows with shutters. Leatherdale's office was on the second floor. Harrow knocked, tried the door, and walked in.

A proper looking young man rose from his desk, blocking Harrow's progress. "Sir, may I help you?"

"Perhaps. My name is John Harrow. I wish to see Mr. Leatherdale."

"I'm afraid Mr. Leartherdale is indisposed today, at home under doctor's care. May I ask your business?"

"What about Mr. Pascual? I understand he is also at this address."

"Oh, I'm afraid Mr. Pascual is rarely here, except for certain legal business. My name is Collins. If it is information you wish ..." Collins the secretary had few actual duties except for what he was doing now. That was running interference from the public. He also sometimes answered the telephone. Kwanyin had chosen him well.

"It's about the Marquis di Paolo estate, you see. I am a small investor, an American visiting London. I had hoped to gain more knowledge, with the prospect of investing a larger sum."

"Oh. I see. Perhaps you should speak to Mr. Kwanyin. He is also an American, a legal consultant for Mr. Pascual. If you will please to be seated, I shall see if he is occupied." He turned and went through a back door.

Harrow was stunned. He dropped into a chair. Of course he knew the name of Kwanyin Luk. DiPaolo had been after him for years. Kwanyin had once tried to kill DiPaolo and nearly succeeded. He had served time in prison, then returned to his crimes. Harrow had no idea the man was involved in this Marquis scheme.

After a few minutes Collins held open the door and Kwanyin entered. "Mr. - Harrow, is it? Please come in. I shall be happy to answer any questions you may have." He smiled. Harrow followed him back to his office and sat by a mahogany desk.

"I understand you are contemplating an investment?"

"Well, yes sir. That is, I already invested a couple hundred. My friends all say I should put in more. But I'd like more assurance this is all on the up and up." Harrow gave a worried smile. Kwanyin laughed.

"I assure you sir, it is. Of course this project entails a great deal of legal work, which runs into money. We also have to pay our genealogists. By the way, have you had your family tree traced yet?"

"Well, no sir, not as such. But I heard my great grandfather was Italian. He came over in—"

Kwanyin waved a hand. "Never mind. If you fill out our proper form, we shall have your genealogy traced free of charge. If it should turn out you have no claim to the di Paolo estate, we shall immediately refund any sums you may have invested. That is our guarantee, sir."

"Ah. Well. I'm relieved to hear that, Mr. Kwan. So do you expect to be paying off pretty soon?"

"Absolutely. Certainly in less than six months from now. The estate has been verified by the Lords and King Commission. They have final say on the matter. It's just a matter of moving things through probate court."

"Well sir, I'm impressed. I never expected a personal guarantee like this. Okay, I'm ready to write you a check for one thousand American dollars right now."

Kwanyin waved a hand. "No hurry, sir. In fact we prefer not to accept personal checks. You should have American Express wire a bank draft, made out to Mr. Pascual. You may wish to deliver it in person. If I'm not here, just leave the draft with Collins. I spend a great deal of time in court, you see. I am responsible for Mr Leatherdale's legal research."

"Oh, all right Mr. Kwan. I will definitely bring a draft here personally tomorrow morning" He rose and extended a hand. "Thank you so much for seeing me today."

Kwanyin smiled again. "My pleasure, sir." Harrow left him still grinning.

Instead of returning to his room, Harrow did go to the American Express office. He wrote a cable to Bernardi that began, I found Kwanyin. He explained what he had done, including how he had managed to withdraw funds from the Marquis di Paolo fund. That part of course was illegal, but only if he were caught. He doubted Kwanyin would complain to Scotland Yard. That might trigger an investigation into his own banking manipulations. Where was this Sr. Pascual, who supposedly owned the account?

Harrow asked Bernardi what he should do. This con should be exposed, but how could he prove anything? More important, how to take Kwanyin into custody? He had not broken any laws in Britain, since that was not where he collected "donations." The U.S. and Britain had as yet no real extradition treaty. Come to that, how could Harrow even prove this was a con? There really had been a Marquis di Paolo who emigrated to England. Whatever became of his estate, if any, was a muddy question. Harrow realized the best he or Bernardi could manage would be to publish an expose', for all the good it might do. He sent off the cable and went back to his hotel to wait. He had fish and chips on Bernardi's expense account.

BERNARDI READ THE CABLE early next morning California time. She sent a brief response—Stay there, find out more if possible. Report daily. B.B. Then she reviewed some other reports she had got from some of her friends in the police department. It appeared there was another local agent now operating openly in San Francisco. It seemed he was authorized to collect donations for the Marquis legal fund. His name was O'Shea, but no one seemed to know much about him. That is, a lot of people knew him from some high toned establishments. But no one knew exactly what he did or where he came from. Or, if they knew, they were not talking. She had been wondering how this Marquis con had made it from London to San Francisco. Now that she knew Kwanyin was involved, it made sense. This city was still the man's real base. She decided on a visit to Mr. O'Shea.

Farmers

An older woman accompanied by a young girl came to collect DiPaolo and Tiago. They communicated by sign language. The two prisoners followed them through the City of Gold to the other side of town, about a mile distant. DiPaolo tried to guess what the total population might add up to. It was hard to estimate. There were small houses built of stone, mud brick, or bamboo. He didn't know how many usually occupied a room. He was struck by the lack of foul smells usually found in American or European cities, with all their horses and bad plumbing. This city had a good sewer system. He noticed a few dogs that looked like wolves.

They arrived at a stone gateway that resembled the one where they had first entered the city. On the other side lay a cleared field free of trees or weeds. It was the first time they had seen empty sky since leaving the river. To one side of the field they saw tall green plants in neat rows. The other side was jungle. The older woman handed them each a farming tool.

"What is this?" DiPaolo turned to Tiago. "I've never seen anything like this."

Tiago turned his over. "I think I have seen pictures. They are used in Peru."

The woman pointed at the empty field, obviously meaning they should get to work. DiPaolo shrugged, pointing at his tool. Impatiently, the woman seized it from him and handed it to the girl, barking a brief order. The girl dropped the basket she had been carrying, took the tool and went to work, demonstrating.

"That's what I thought," Tiago said. "It's a foot plow." He nodded at the woman and went to work beside the girl. Reluctantly, DiPaolo took his back from the girl and started work with Tiago. It proved to be hard labor, but not as hard as using a pick and shovel would have been. DiPaolo imitated what he had watched the girl do and what Tiago was doing. The tool was a long curved wooden pole, curved forward to provide a lever. At the bottom it had a short peg sticking from the side. The end held a sharp metal blade.

DiPaolo went to work. He stepped on the foot peg, driving the blade deep into the earth. Then he pulled back on the upper end so that the blade gouged out a divot of earth. Put the blade in again and repeat. It worked like a plow. After a few minutes Tiago began working faster, once he got the hang of it. DiPaolo found it hard, but he could see how two men could plow a field almost as fast as one man and a mule. After a few minutes sweat dripped from his brow. He took his shirt off and kept plowing.

The young girl handed them a jar of water. They drank and kept working. DiPaolo lost track of time.

When the sun was high the woman stopped them. They sat on the ground while she passed out a type of hard bread and some sweet berries. DiPaolo had never found food more delicious. He pointed at the foot plows and said to Tiago, "Those blades are made of bronze. Where do they get it?"

Tiago shrugged. "The scholars think they know all about this land. They know nothing."

"You seem to know more, Tiago. You are the first camarata I have met who can read and write. How is that?"

Tiago said, "Missionaries. I was forced to go to school. I escaped when I could, but not before I was infected with religion and knowledge. I still read books when I can."

DiPaolo said, "If we ever get out of this place I shall see you get many books."

Tiago smiled. "If."

They worked most of the day. DiPaolo at the end felt exhausted, but he could still walk. He was surprised to feel as well as he did. There was plenty of food and the mosquitoes for once were not tormenting him. On the way back the girl left them, but the woman made them take a short detour. They came to a canal with swiftly flowing water. The woman stopped and pointed expectantly.

"What does she want?"

Tiago shrugged. "I'm not sure, but—"

The woman gave him a shove toward the canal. He said, "Oh. I see." He had already abandoned his shirt. Now he dropped his pants and plunged into the canal. After a moment DiPaolo followed.

It felt wonderful to wash off the filth of weeks.

THERE FOLLOWED SEVERAL days of the same routine. Brazil, in the tropical zone, could grow crops year round. The only danger arose from extreme heat. When a waxing moon rose they began working at night, sometimes most of it, until DiPaolo lost his sense of time. How many days had he been in this city? At least they ate well. What crops the gardens could not provide was supplied by hunting and gathering. They dined on fresh fish from the river, including enormous catfish, and sometimes piranha. Tiago cooked some himself in their room's fire pit. DiPaolo worked loose the soles of his rotting boots and used the leather laces to fashion a usable pair of sandals.

The girl who always accompanied them to the fields seemed to be taking an interest in Tiago. During their few breaks she spoke to him in her own language. He smiled and replied with what vocabulary he had learned. He told DiPaolo the girl's name was Runs in Rain. The old woman stood by watching them converse. Her face bore a stern expression, but she didn't try to interfere.

Then one morning DiPaolo, lulled to sleepiness, had a sudden sense of coming awake. What was he doing here? He got the sense Tiago would be content to remain, spending the remainder of his life in this city. Already Tiago had learned enough of the language to begin communicating at a basic level. DiPaolo realized he himself had drifted into a sense of security. He no longer felt in daily fear of his life, as he had on Roosevelt's expedition. His health had improved, he ate well and gained weight. And yet he could not imagine remaining here. He wanted to return to San Francisco and his Benita Bernardi. He wanted to wear civilized clothing again, to ride a streetcar, read books, go to theaters. Run his detective agency. He had left Jack Harrow in charge. How was the man doing? DiPaolo felt dazed, thinking. There had to be a way to escape this city.

Over the next few days he talked to Tiago about his thoughts. Tiago might have told someone else. Kerkan came to see them. He said, "You will not have work today. There is to be a trial."

DiPaolo felt a sense of dread. Now what? "What kind of trial? What have we done?"

Kerkan said, "There is still disagreement among the chiefs. Some say your coming here was meant by the spirits. But we do not know if it is for good or evil. Some say you should be killed. Others, that you be allowed to remain. Still others that you be sent back. There has not been such conflict among the chiefs in our memory."

Tiago glanced at DiPaolo, who had turned pale. Tiago said, "So we are to be put on trial? On the platform, like last time?"

"No." Kerkan studied them a moment. "It is to be a trial of your spirits. To see if you are good or evil. Or perhaps neither. You must fast until tomorrow night. Then the trial shall begin. Do not go outside, speak to no one. You may drink water. No food." Then, abruptly, Kerkan turned and left the hut.

DiPalo took a deep breath. He said, "What do you make of that?"

Tiago shook his head. "There are still many things I don't know about this place. I try to ask the Indians. I don't yet speak their tongue well. Nor do they seem eager to tell me anything. Maybe this will be some trial of combat, or where we're forced to walk through hot coals in our bare feet."

DiPaolo winced. "I think I'd prefer the combat. If they allow us weapons."

Their guards had long since disappeared from their door. DiPaolo considered making a run for it. But he knew he wouldn't get far in that jungle without a guide. There was nowhere to escape to. He couldn't even tell north from south. That night he awakened to overhear Tiago quietly reciting a prayer in Brazilian.

O'Shea

O"Shea had enough business these days to hire his own secretary. Some downtown offices were beginning to hire more women, which seemed like not a bad idea. A nice looking lady could act as a good buffer zone between himself and upset clients. O'Shea took on a woman he had met at one of the parlor houses he sometimes visited. She was a little old for that kind of work, but she knew how to manage. She didn't need to take dictation or type, just talk to clients, answer the phone and sometimes file. He called her Miss Gwen, not knowing her actual name. O'Shea wasn't sure how much she understood about the con, but he knew she could keep her mouth shut. He paid her well.

Miss Gwen knocked once on his office door, poked her head in. "Lady to see you, sir."

He looked up in surprise. Not many women came to see him, at least not alone. He gestured for Miss Gwen to come in, closing the door behind her. He asked in a low tone, "Anybody you know? What's she like?"

Miss Gwen shrugged. "She looks familiar, but I can't place her." Miss Gwen only called him <u>sir</u> when there was someone else around. "She looks well off, though. Wears a fur wrap and a couple diamonds."

O'Shea scented a possible mark. He licked his dry lips. He had been going through daily receipts and expenses. This sounded more interesting. "She give a name?"

"Mrs. Riley." Irish. That helped place her in O'Shea's mind. San Francisco held a balance of power between Catholics (divided between Irish and Italians), Jews, and Protestants. The Irish ran the police and fire department. Italians had the Bank of Italy among other assets. The other two groups shared what was left, including City Hall.

O'Shea said, "Show her in. Tell her I'm real busy, but I'm making an exception. Because we're both Irish." O'Shea, of course, was nothing of the sort.

Miss Gwen escorted Mrs. Riley to the inner sanctum. O'Shea rose to greet her, extending a hand. She ignored the hand and glanced over his office, as if about to find fault with his housekeeping. He said, "Please, Mrs. Riley. How may I be of service?"

She took a seat at the other side of the desk and rearranged her mink. Of course she wore white gloves. She opened a handbag and withdrew a folded paper after rummaging a few seconds. The handbag was huge and covered with gllittering fake jewels. She said, "It's about this Marquis di Paolo business. I am certain I am not descended from the Marquis. There are no Italians in my family. But I am given to understand you are selling shares in this affair."

He cleared his throat. If this were a man he would have immediately offered whiskey. He wasn't sure about Mrs. Riley. She might be a tea totaler, one of those Temperance women. He said, "That is true, Mrs. Riley. We do sell a limited number of shares. The di Paolo estate project will involve two or three billion dollars when finally settled. In the meantime, we must raise funds for legal expenses in Britain. We therefore offer shares, currently at the rate of twenty-five dollars each. We guarantee an ultimate return of five hundred dollars for each dollar invested. Of course, the share price may be increased at any time. May I ask if you are considering an investment?"

She sniffed. "Your rate of return sounds too good to be true. My attorney advises me to be cautious."

O'Shea chuckled. "I quite agree. You are free to check out our credentials. Our case is currently pending a trial date in the London court. You will find we are on the up and up, as they say." He smiled.

Mrs. Riley did not smile. She unfolded the paper she had been holding. "I received this notice in my mail yesterday. It describes the case in some detail. Now, when Mr. Riley passed away six months ago, he left me everything. He owned a construction company, you see. I have been searching for a suitable investment plan."

"Ah. I am terribly sorry, madam, to hear of your dear husband. As your attorney says, you should be cautious. Perhaps you might consider purchasing just one or two shares of our enterprise at first. Later, you may invest more if it seems wise."

"Yes, but what if the case should go against you? Will my investment be refunded?"

O'Shea realized his hand had been fiddling with a pencil, rolling it between his fingers. He put it down. This mark was ready to fall, he could sense it. "Oh, well, I shouldn't worry, madam. Our legal case is iron clad. We can't possibly lose, though of course these things always take time. All that legal rigamarole and so on. But yes, if the inconceivable should somehow come about and we lose the case, every penny invested will be happily refunded. That is our guarantee."

Mrs. Riley looked over the office again. O'Shea got the feeling she thought it looked a little seedy. He would have to do something about that. Call in a decorator. He started to say something else but she interrupted.

"Very well, sir. I am prepared to make an initial investment. I shall make out a check for one hundred dollars."

"Ah. Well, I am glad to hear this. But I must caution we do not accept personal drafts. Here, I shall provide a stamped, addressed envelope. Please go to your bank and obtain a counter check. Or a postal money order. That is more secure all around." He didn't add that she would receive no canceled check to prove she had ever paid. Just four share certificates.

Mrs. Riley abruptly rose, snapping shut her handbag. "I shall certainly do so at once, Mr. O'Shea. Thank you for seeing me today, I know you are busy. I am glad we had this conversation. Good day to you, sir."

"My pleasure, madam." He saw her to the door. When she was gone, Miss Gwen stopped him on his way back. She said, "I remember where I saw her before."

"Oh?" He paused, mildly curious. "Where was that?"

"I saw her picture in the papers a few times. And once at the Policeman's Ball. Her name isn't Riley. It's Benita Bernardi."

BERNARDI WENT FROM there directly to the office of the DiPaolo Detective Agency. She found the agent named Robert in a back room where he kept his desk and files. His office was more cluttered than the others, and littered with strange scientific measuring devices including some bottles of mysterious chemicals. Bernardi opened her handbag. She said, "I think it worked. There was plenty of light in that office."

Paul took the bag, reached inside and unscrewed something. He took out a small black box. "You're sure you kept the lens clear?"

"Of course." One of the glass diamonds on the side of the bag was really a camera lens. Paul said,

"I'll take this to the darkroom. The negative will have to wash and dry before I can make a print. You might want to come back in an hour or so."

She handed him a stamped and addressed business envelope. "I also got his fingerprints, if that's much use."

He slipped on a pair of rubber gloves, took the envelope and filed it. He made sure to write down the date, time, and place of collection. "You never know. The courts started accepting fingerprints as legal evidence two years ago, back in Chicago. This might turn out to be valuable."

Bernardi had one of the other detectives escort her to lunch, which of course she paid for. In the restaurant she looked over the few other upper class ladies in the room. She decided the outfit she was wearing was out of style. She must do something about that. She was glad she'd left the mink behind.

When she returned to the office, Paul held up a small photo, using tongs. The print was still wet. He said, "Pretty good image. I can have it enlarged and made into flyers if you like."

She squinted at the photograph. O'Shea's grinning face stared out at her. It was mostly in good focus. She said, "That's a great little camera you made."

He shrugged. "I just modified a Kodak. I think I could make one even better."

"This is good enough for now. There's no need for flyers. Just make me a few copies. We're going to show them around the police station and some other places. Someone may know who he is."

And, she thought, that knowledge may lead to his connection with Kwanyin Luk.

Trial

In the evening just at sunset they came for the prisoners. Kergan led a party of two men and a woman, all of them about Kergan's age. They wore feathers, beads, and body paint. DiPaolo had for a moment the absurd idea they were wearing formal dress, like attorneys or judges in a court of law. Perhaps it was the way they looked at him. Kergan said, "It is time. You come."

Without a word they followed. Kergan led them to a street that passed around the central pyramid to the other side. There they found a low, round structure covered by a dome. There was a single entrance at one side. DiPaolo found his voice. "Is this to be a trial by combat? Or by fire?" He dreaded the answer. Kergan said,

"It is a trial by light. You enter now." He pointed to the dark doorway. Tiago entered first, followed by DiPaolo. He found himself descending a short ladder into a circular chamber. A single burning rush light stood at one side. The three others entered after DiPaolo. Kergan motioned for Tiago and DiPaolo to sit. Then he used the rush light to kindle a small fire at the center of the chamber. When it was burning well, the woman took some leaves from a bag and sprinkled them on the flames. A pungent odor filled the air, sweet and sharp. The woman began to chant.

She chanted some tuneless song for a minute or two. She stopped and one of the men took up the story, whatever it was. DiPaolo understood not a word, but he could hear the meter and noted repeated words and phrases. When the first had finished the other man chanted as well, for several minutes. DiPaolo glanced at Tiago, wondering how much he understood, if any. Tiago gave no sign.

Kerkan said, "The priests pray to spirits to reveal truth. You will take the medicine now. I leave you. I return when the trial is done." He turned, went up the ladder and disappeared into the night. DiPaolo asked of no one, "What medicine?" His question was answered when the woman handed him an earthen cup. It contained some bitter-smelling tea. She motioned for him to drink.

For a moment DiPaolo considered refusing, then realized he would have no choice. At least he didn't have to walk on hot coals. He choked down the foul-tasting brew and handed back the cup. The woman refilled it from a jar and passed it to Tiago. Tiago gave DiPaolo a smile and drank his portion down.

"What now?" DiPaolo asked. "Is that poison?" No one answered.

DiPaolo decided he might as well relax. The tea, whatever it was, had not made him sick at least yet. He had eaten nothing for more than twenty-four hours. He should have been hungry. In fact he had felt hunger before drinking the brew, though he would have said he had no appetite. No, he just felt relaxed. The three priests did nothing but sit and tend the fire. DiPaolo stretched out on the floor and stared at the dark ceiling, waiting for whatever would happen next.

The woman began to hum to herself. No words, only soft musical tones. DiPaolo had slept little the previous night. He realized he was tired. But he kept his eyes open and bit his tongue, determined to remain awake. Then he fell asleep.

Fell was the right word. He felt a moment of dreaming panic, falling into a dark pit. He felt himself spinning as if going down in a deep spiral. Utter blackness surrounded him. He tried to scream but could find no breath. DiPaolo was aware he was dreaming, but could not control it. He remembered being told somewhere that if a person dreams of falling and hits the ground he dies. He felt utter terror.

Then he struck bottom, except it was not ground. It was like a thin membrane or curtain. He burst through into light.

Now it was a different dream. He floated in the sky. Somewhere in the distance he heard a musical tone, rising and falling. He remembered the woman's soft hum. He could not puzzle if it was the same. The sky filled with light, without clouds, free of shadows. He had never seen such brightness, like staring at the sun. He spread his arms and felt that he could fly. There was no earth below, no bottom, only empty shining sky. He felt a deep confusion in his mind, whether to be terrified or filled with joy. And yet his mind still functioned at another level. He wondered how he had come to be here. Was it from his own choice, or because of some abstract force called fate? He had never believed in that, and yet some primeval instinct made him sense its presence.

He landed on something. In an instant the dome of bright sky vanished and he found himself in a sort of cavern lighted by flickering torches that he could not see. He stood naked on hard rocky ground, a stone roof not far above. Some human form came forward from the darkness, from the depths of the cave. Somehow he felt no surprise on seeing Benita Bernardi. She looked at him with the cool, appraising gaze she often had, from about six feet away. He waited for her to speak. She said,

"What do you do here, Martino?"

He sucked in a deep breath, realizing he had been holding it. He said, "I don't know. I didn't want to come here."

"Then why did you go with Roosevelt? You could have died on the river. You might have chosen to remain at home with me. Comfortable and warm."

He said without thinking, "I wanted to see. This is a place I have not been. And I did not want to do less than Roosevelt. The man has courage. I needed to test myself."

She nodded, seeming to think. She said, "And now you have seen. You have learned. You have courage and you are tested. Why do you remain?"

He raised both hands, helpless. "I could not find my way, even if they let me go. I am a prisoner."

She said, "No, Martino. You are a prisoner only in your mind. I need you at home. There are troubles. Come home to me." And abruptly she vanished.

DiPalo felt more confused than ever. He was alone in a dark cavern. The music he had heard earlier was gone. In the cavern was utter silence. It was not the first time he had been underground. He had been in several deep mines during the course of his past detective work. There was always the silence. After a time you would begin to think you heard things, people whispering in the distance, or the rocks themselves making strange noises. He hated underground.

Another person approached, from a different direction. When the figure drew closer DiPaolo recognized him. It was Kwanyin Luk. DiPaolo found no surprise in seeing this man. DiPaolo knew Benita loved him. This man hated him. All was in balance. He said, "What do you want, Luk?"

Kwanyin came no closer, though DiPaolo half expected him to attack. Kwanyin said, "You are a coward. You let a woman run you. She runs your agency, she runs your life. She tries to attack me, but will fail. I am too strong now. Why not return and fight me yourself? I have missed you, Martino."

DiPaolo had no idea what Kwanyin meant by Benita attacking him, but he would not be surprised if she did. He said, "If I can return I shall, Kwanyin. I have missed you too."

Then he fell through the floor, into a deep pool of spinning, bright colors. For a time, he lost his mind.

Pascual

Kwanyin found it necessary to take on another of his personas, that of Juan C.T. Pascual, legal executor for the Marquis estate. He composed a letter to be copied and mailed to all prospective heirs. It explained that Leatherdale had filed a new appeal in the London probate court. Unfortunately it might take up to six months to work its way through the legal system. "We beg your patience. Please recall that the Marquis estate continues to gather compound interest. The longer the settlement is delayed, the greater the amount that will be rewarded." Kwanyin included with the letter a copy of Leatherdale's legal brief including his signature. It even bore a rubber stamp showing the date filed. Kwanyin himself almost believed it.

He was still furious about the money DiPaolo had somehow stolen from his accounts. He still did not understand exactly how it was done. It was a criminal act, and yet he could prove nothing without making himself vulnerable to law enforcement. He would need to take steps to insure it could not happen again. The only way was to diversify the accounts. Rather than keeping the Marquis funds in his own private account, he would have to divide it among his several agents in the States. Each would have a joint account with himself and would require his approval for any withdrawal. Kwanyin cursed the extra paperwork this would involve. Eventually he must travel to Switzerland to open a central account there. As soon as he had time.

He wondered why DiPaolo had not cleaned out the account when he had the chance. He had withdrawn two hundred thousand and left the remainder, close to a hundred thousand at the time. Kwanyin suspected this had been part of an old pickpocket con. When you lift a mark's wallet, you take most of the cash but leave some. Then return the wallet. When the mark checks, he sees the money and thinks he wasn't robbed because, after all, wouldn't a thief take everything? That made Kwanyin even angrier. It was as if DiPaolo was insulting him by treating him like another mark.

Kwanyin, months before, had come up with the idea for this scheme when by accident he had seen the name of the Marquis di Paolo in some historical magazine article. The man really existed, and was wealthy in his time. Why not use the name for a grand estate con? It could prove the ultimate insult to Martino, and at the same time might even succeed in drawing him into a trap.

Where was DiPaolo anyway? Why had he pretended to go off with Roosevelt? That afternoon Kwanyin got off a cable to O'Shea in San Francisco. *Get some boys to keep an eye out for DiPaolo. I want to know what he's doing.*

JACK HARROW, PER BERNARDI'S instructions, remained in London. However, he didn't think of this as vacation. He got his notes together and wrote up a formal report. At American Express he paid to have several copies typed up. Then he went to visit the American consul. He got in to see him after waiting only three days. He dropped a copy of his report on the man's desk.

"It's all there," he said. The consul wore an old fashioned suit with tails. He also sported a handlebar mustache. Harrow guessed he was trying to pass himself off as a Victorian. But he had been appointed by Wilson and had a Southern accent.

"What's all there?"

"A major case of fraud. Have you heard of the Marquis di Paolo estate?"

The consul glanced at the report on his desk with an expression as if he were looking at a dead mouse. "I've heard of it. There are a lot of frauds these days. Look at the patent medicine ads. Not much we can do about them."

Harrow pulled up a chair without invitation and sat down, leaning across the desk. "This scheme is pulling in hundreds of thousands of American dollars. It's supposed to be run by Leatherdale and Pascual, but the man really behind it is an American named Kwanyin Luk."

"Don't sound American."

"Chinese American by way of Hong Kong English. The man has a complicated past. The point is, he's committing massive mail fraud. The U.S. Postal Service knows about him. I made sure of that. They would like to get their hands on him." The fact was, Harrow had just sent a copy of his report to Postal inspectors in Washington a few days earlier. He had not yet received a reply. But he was betting he would. That was one government department that actually worked.

The consul picked up Harrow's report and dropped it again. "I'll read this later, Mr. Harrow. But I'm afraid there's nothing I can do. This person has broken no laws in Britain that he could be arrested for. And we have no extradition at present."

"You could have him deported. Will you at least contact Scotland Yard? Express your concerns?"

A broad smile. "I shall certainly do my best, Mr. Harrow. Now, if you will excuse me, I do have an important engagement." He got to his feet. Harrow took the hint and got out.

Back in his room, Harrow considered his options. Of course he had committed a major crime himself when he forged access to Kwanyin's American bank account. Kwanyin would have to go to the U.S. to pursue the matter, and that he would not do. Harrow had left some money in the account because he didn't want Kwanyin to close it. It was still sitting there with Kwanyin's marks all over it. The fact that it existed was proof of fraud. Harrow also wanted to confuse the man.

If this was the work of an outside thief, why not take all the cash? Kwanyin would begin to suspect others in his little empire. Harrow decided to wait for developments. He had tossed a rock in a pond. Now he would see where the ripples went.

BENITA BERNARDI LOOKED at her bank statement with growing concern. Two hundred thousand was a great deal of money. How was she to explain it, if someone were to begin asking questions? Harrow should be sending in his weekly report and expense account soon. She prayed he would not mention this particular deal. Nor did she intend to ask how he'd done it. She decided for her own peace of mind to rid herself of all this capital. She knew the money had come from the di Paolo estate victims. If she had any way to return it she would. But even if she had their names and addresses, probably most of them would insist on Kwanyin's keeping the money. An investment of a lifetime.

She would donate all that cash to several charities, starting with the Policeman's Benevolent Association. She wished Martino were here.

IN LONDON, KWANYIN went to visit Leatherdale at his flat. The barrister had stopped coming to his office unless Kwanyin brought him there. He seldom went out and seemed to spend most of his time reading the same books over and over. The doctors all said his physical health was fine, but his mind was slipping. An elderly lady was there to watch over him. Kwanyin had never bothered to learn her name. He sat down opposite Leatherdale, who occupied an easy chair by the window.

"How are you, sir?"

Leatherdale put down his book and smiled. "Well enough, thank you. You are Mr. Pascual, aren't you?"

That was good. The barrister remembered him. He said, "Has anyone else been to see you recently, Mr. Leathedale? Any strangers?"

Leathedale gave a vacant look, shook his head. "None that I recall. Why do you ask? Am I to expect new clients? I'm quite busy now with my current cases, you see. I'm not sure I have time to take on a new case."

"No sir, I shouldn't worry about that. I just wondered." He turned to the caretaker, who hovered in the doorway, a feather duster in one hand. She guessed his question and answered.

"No sir, no strangers have come to see the master. A few of his old friends used to drop by now and then, but they have mostly stopped coming. It is most sad."

"Indeed it is. Perhaps someone from his parish might be willing to come by once or twice a week."

"Mr. Leatherdale has never been the religious sort far as I know. But I should be happy to inquire."

"Yes, please do that. I have made out a check here for his usual household expenses. I have included a small rise in your own salary."

She bobbed a small curtsey. "Thank you, sir."

As he left, Kwanyin felt a genuine regret for Leatherdale's condition. He had been a brilliant attorney at one time. Kwanyin wished he could do more for him. Besides, if the man died Kwanyin would have to find a new front man.

That afternoon he made a decision. His own problems were traceable to Martino DiPaolo. Kwanyin had heard from O'Shea. He knew about Benita Bernardi's snooping. That could only be DiPaolo's doing. He had put her up to it. No woman would be so clever or daring on her own. DiPaolo was staying out of sight, on the pretext he was actually off on some adventure in Peru. But he must be there, in San Francisco. Hiding out for his own reasons, whatever they might be. He was causing trouble once again. Kwanyin had once tried to kill him and nearly succeeded. He should have shot him two or three times instead of only once.

Despite the dangers, he would have to travel again to the States. He must not trust anyone else to carry out this job. Besides, he needed to do it himself for his own peace of mind. He would go to San Francisco and kill DiPaolo

Going

DiPaolo came to himself lying on the ground in a park-like square, surrounded with alien shrubs bearing strange flowers. The flowers were of all colors and seemed to glow even in daylight. He did not know how he had come here, whether by walking or being carried. Had he been asleep? He seemed to remember a dream. He had looked at the nearby mountains and remarked how beautiful they were. He turned to one side and saw the ocean's water, equally beautiful, and said so. Someone nearby, an Indian woman, answered. She said,

"Yes. This place is always more beautiful than the real world."

He said, "How do you know this is not the real world?"

She answered, "Because it never changes here. When you return next time it will be the same. The real world changes all the time." Then the dream ended. He sat up. Tiago was next to him, also sitting, staring into space as if thinking. DiPaolo started to say something to him, then realized he had nothing to say.

Kerkan was there. He brought them back to their hut, where a woman waited with water and food.

The next day no one came to escort them to the tilled field. Plowing was almost done, and they expected to begin the planting. Yet no one came that day. DiPaolo left the hut, no one tried to stop him. He walked up and down the street for a time, watching people. Women cared for small children, others went by with baskets of food or other supplies on their backs. Down the street some men were laying bricks. DiPaolo grew nervous he might get lost too far from his hut, so he turned back. No one came. Someone had left them enough food and water to last a day or two. Tiago sat quietly cross-legged, watching out the door, saying nothing. DiPaolo thought of beginning a conversation, then realized he still had nothing to say. He remembered his dream. He wondered if Tiago had also dreamed. But he would not ask.

A day after that, Kerkan came to them. He told them to gather their possessions and to pack their knapsacks. But he said, "Only those things you came here with. Take nothing you found here."

DiPaolo glanced at the water jar. It was a fine piece of decorated ceramic work. He wanted to keep it. But he left it where it lay. He said, "What is to happen now, Lord Kerkan?"

He said, "The chiefs have decided. When you were in the dream, you were questioned. You do not remember, but you answered all questions, speaking truth. Still, the chiefs disagreed. Some said you should not be allowed to leave. Two thought you should be killed. In the end, it was decided to let you go. You were brought here to discover the reason your men are in the forest, on the river. The chiefs are satisfied with your answers. The spirits say you must be free. Take up your bundles now. You are to leave at once, if you wish. You will be guided in the forest."

DiPaolo lifted his bag. He was ready. In the time he had been here he had been able to mend and patch what clothing he had, but he wore now only shorts and sandals. If he was really to be let go, he would not pause to change. He glanced at Tiago. Tiago turned to Kerkan and spoke a few words in the native tongue. Kerkan nodded and made a gesture with both hands. DiPaolo said, "What did you tell him, Tiago?"

Tiago turned to DiPaolo and held out a hand. He said, "I told him I wish to stay. He said I can."

Kerkan, to Tiago, "There is a woman you may marry. I will bring you to her. She has seen you and admires. You have seen her, the one who carried food when you were plowing. She is Runs in Rain. She would choose you as husband." Then, to DiPaolo, "You may leave. There is but one condition. You must never speak of this city to anyone outside. Swear it."

DiPaolo swallowed. That was a great deal to ask. How could he not speak of this place? And yet, if he had honor, he must keep an oath. He raised a hand. "I swear I shall not speak of this place." Already his mind was racing. Did that include not writing of it? He pushed the thought aside. Kerkan pointed to the door. Tiago gripped DiPaolo's hand a moment, then embraced him. DiPaolo said, "Farewell, old friend." Then Tiago was gone.

Kerkan touched DiPaolo's arm to stop him from following. He held out a leather pouch. He said, "The chiefs agreed you should have this. It is a reminder to keep secret this city, if you choose to leave." DiPaolo took the pouch. It was heavier than it looked. He opened it, removed the object inside, and gave a little gasp.

"My god, this is worth a fortune." He held a disk about three inches in diameter, covered with fine engravings in an unknown script. He had no doubt it was pure gold.

"Put it on," Kerkan said. The disk was connected to a gold chain. DiPaolo slipped it around his neck and under his shirt.

Kerkan said, "If you are faithful to your oath it will protect you from evil. Now goodbye." He turned and left the hut. DiPaolo followed.

Two warriors awaited him. They were mostly naked and each carried only a small bag as well as a war club. One had a bronze dagger at his belt. DiPaolo longed to ask him where he had got it, but it was too late to begin learning the language. They set off at once into the rain forest, leaving by way of the same arched entrance where Tiago and DiPaolo had entered. Somehow they found a trail invisible to DiPaolo's eyes. They moved at a fast walk, nearly a run, never breaking so much as a twig. One man stayed ahead, the other behind DiPaolo. They ran for what seemed hours, until DiPaolo, exhausted, tripped and fell. The two men stopped and waited for him to rise, without helping.

DiPaolo made a gesture like drinking. He had not brought a canteen, nor did they carry water. One of them made a sign that DiPaolo saw as meaning *wait,* then disappeared into the jungle. DiPaolo sat down to wait. The other man merely watched. About ten minutes later the first warrior returned bearing a water skin dripping with moisture. He passed it to DiPaolo, who quickly swallowed, nearly choking. As he handed it back, he realized he could hear somewhere the sound of flowing water. They must be near the river.

That night they camped in a small clearing without a fire. They shared some pieces of dry bread, then simply lay down and slept. No one kept watch. DiPaolo found the ground cloth in his back pack and slept on that, regardless of bugs. He was too tired not to sleep.

Leaving London

J ack Harrow wasn't being idle, waiting for Kwanyin to make a move. It had proved easy to find out where the man was living in London. He had needed only to ask a few questions of Leatherdale's caregiver. Then he had found a way to meet James, Kwanyin's valet. He lived most of the time in Kwanyin's suite at one of London's better hotels - one that tolerated a few Orientals, as long as they could pay. On his days off, or when Kwanyin was out of town, James kept another household in the East End. He never traveled with his employer. The other household consisted of a fortyish widow with two teen age sons. Harrow didn't know if they were James's boys, but it didn't seem to matter. They were in school most of the time when they weren't roaming the streets.

Harrow managed to meet James in the hotel's cafe. Kwanyin was out somewhere, so James had little to do, though he was expected to be there when his employer returned. Londoners, especially posh valets, are supposed to be private and proper. James wasn't. Harrow had no problem offering to buy him a drink. He presented himself as an American business agent trying to get to know England, learning the customs and so on.

After two drinks, James said, "Forget London. Go back home. I've often thought of emigrating myself, maybe to Australia. London smothers one."

That led to a conversation about working conditions. It soon appeared that James despised his current employer, Kwanyin Luk. "It's not I'm against the Chinee, that ain't the problem. And he pays me proper. But I don't think he's all he says he is. I don't know what all he's up to, but I suspect it ain't all on the level. Sometimes I hear him use different names on the tellyphone. Pascual is one."

"Really. How interesting." Harrow let the man talk. In the end, Harrow recruited James as a spy. Harrow made up some excuse for wanting to know more because of personal business reasons. James would keep Harrow informed of Kwanyin's movements, or anything else that might interest him. Harrow put James on a "retainer." James looked pleased with the idea.

Thus it was that Harrow learned more than he expected to know. James would leave a note at the end of each day in the hotel's outbox. Harrow would drop by to pick it up. Most of the messages contained unimportant information, such as times when Kwanyin went out or came back, or if he said where he was going. He did not make many phone calls, but several times called American Express to dictate cables to O'Shea in the States. Evidently there was a great deal of money being passed back and forth. One detail was a mailing address in New York, where "donations" were to be sent. Harrow made a note to check that out when he could.

Then he learned that Kwanyin was traveling back to the States. He felt like a hound who has just caught the scent of blood.

KWANYIN PREPARED CAREFULLY for the trip. One problem was that he had no one he could trust to handle the London business in his absence. He might have to remain in the States for several weeks. He should have taken steps to remedy this months earlier. The best he could do at this point would be to have any mail forwarded to his New York address. Cablegrams could be redirected through American Express to wherever he found himself. By this time he had thirty deputies working for him in the States, handling correspondence and donations. O'Shea had recruited some of them, some others Kwanyin, in the role of "Pascual", had enlisted by mail. A few of them were in on the con, but most were sincere believers. They were loyal to the Marquis di Paolo estate and would not dream of betraying it.

His valet, James, he kept on a modest salary to maintain his apartment and to handle any minor business, such as donors looking for information on how to contact Pascual. He was instructed where to forward any personal mail.

All those details arranged, Kwanyin decided on a new persona. Being Oriental, he could never pass as Italian. But people usually see what they expect to see. In San Francisco he had spent some time masquerading as a Hindu seer, wearing a turban. He might pass as an American Indian if need be. And he had no problem being Russian, descended from the Mongol Horde. Since the revolution, there were a good many Russians showing up in Europe. Kwanyin took care to select the right kind of clothing, the expensive kind that might suggest him somehow related to the Romanoffs. A convincing diamond stickpin and some other jewelry completed the illusion. He went so far as to purchase a Russian phrasebook and begin learning a few common sentences.

His preparations took only about two weeks. He purchased a first class cabin on a Star liner. One of the few items bought prior to departure was a new American revolver, a Police Special. He needed only one steamer trunk.

JACK HARROW NEVER LOST sight of the quarry. He didn't know about Kwanyin's disguise, since Kwanyin had never revealed it to James. But James knew he was leaving, and on what ship. James had offered to accompany him to the wharf, but Kwanyin for some reason declined. That morning a modestly dressed Chinese gentleman left London. He stopped at a private club long enough to change clothes. A rough-edged semi-wealthy Russian boarded a steamship. Jack Harrow was already aboard.

They were at sea five days. Harrow, in second class, spent most of his time in his cabin. He swore he would never get aboard another ship. He made a few ventures on deck trying to spot Kwanyin, but failed. Likely they would not cross paths if the quarry was in first class. The third day out he did get to see the ship's purser. Harrow presented his credentials as a "special police agent" which was code for private detective. The purser was impressed enough, after some convincing, to allow Harrow to see the passenger list. Harrow read it carefully. There were over four hundred names, but only fifty-three in first class. No Kwanyin. Harrow turned to the purser. He was an old sailor with a Scots accent. Harrow said,

"All sorts of names here. I assume you have met all the first class passengers. Perhaps in the dining room. Any of them strike you as foreign? Orientals perhaps?"

A shrug. "A couple of Anglo-Indians there, husband and spouse. The only one with an accent I recall would be the Russian. Anton Zharov." He pointed at the name.

"Huh." Harrow closed the book. "Thank you, sir. I'm afraid this doesn't help much. But if my man is aboard, I'm sure I'll find him somehow."

He returned to his cabin. Kwanyin might be traveling in second class or even steerage. No one would be surprised at a Chinese in steerage provided he had a visa for entry. The Chinese exclusion act had been passed years ago. But Kwanyin had citizenship. He could come and go. Harrow had a plan in case he did manage to find him on board. He would present himself as one of the di Paolo estate petitioners. *What a coincidence to meet Kwanyin here. Did he remember him from London? He surely hoped so.* It could have been a great chance to pump more information out of the man.

But now he felt as if he were following the trail of an invisible person.

KWANYIN AKA ZHAROV for his part enjoyed the voyage. He became instantly a celebrity among first class passengers. They wanted to hear all about his experiences in St. Petersburg during the revolution and his adventures since then. Did he really know the Romanovs? Such a terrible, sad story. For his part he spun a tale of escaping the Bolsheviks by sewing diamonds and rubies into his clothes and boarding a fishing boat in the Black Sea.

He even revealed that he was now heavily invested in the DiPaolo estate project. Of course he was not a descendant and could not inherit, but he had purchased many shares. They were guaranteed to pay off once the lawsuit was settled. Probably in the next three months or so. He had this inside information from Leatherdale and Pascual themselves. Perhaps the passenger he was speaking to might be interested? Zharov was authorized to accept donations to exchange for legal shares. He actually sold several shares, personally signed by himself, Anton Zharov, for several hundred dollars. Of course, he explained these were not purchases in a legal sense. They were donations. Shares of the estate were given freely. Thus there could be no question of illegal market trading.

This voyage was paying for itself. He thanked his good luck there had been no actual Russians aboard.

Return

DiPaolo wondered where these two warriors were taking him. Of course he could not ask since their only communication was by sign language. He wished he had questioned Kerkan before leaving the City of Gold, but events had happened too quickly. One day he was in fear of execution, the next he was set free and taken to the forest. The second day's trek proved a little easier than the first. He guessed they had done twenty miles the first day. The second was perhaps fifteen. One of the warriors spotted a monkey in a tree. He drew a bolo from his pouch, tossed it, and that afternoon they had monkey meat roasted on a spit. It was the only time he saw them smile.

The third day of the trek began at dawn as usual. At first they moved fast, as if in a rush. At about noon the lead warrior halted briefly and pointed at something ahead. DiPaolo could not make out even the trail, much less what the man was pointing at. The other Indian spoke one word and they moved on, but more slowly. DiPaolo wondered if they were finally about to find the river. If they were below the rapids he might build a small raft to float downstream. He could only hope. An hour or two later he heard a strange sound, the murmur of distant voices. They sounded somehow familiar. He could not make out words, but the rhythm of speech sounded Brazilian. They could not possibly be Roosevelt's party. DiPaolo and Tiago had been gone for weeks. DiPaolo had lost track of time, but he guessed it might be two months. The expedition, if it still existed, must be home by now, or nearly so.

They came to an abrupt halt. DiPaolo stopped, wondering what was wrong. He had been concentrating on watching the trail, where his feet went, what lay ahead. Now he realized the murmur of voices was louder. He could smell the smoke of a campfire and the aroma of cooking meat. He couldn't stop himself from drooling.

The leading Indian spoke one word. Or rather he barked it. He pointed ahead, through the curtain of trees and brush. DiPaolo understood. He hefted his knapsack and stepped through, out of the jungle. Into the campsite of the Roosevelt expedition.

For several minutes no one noticed him. The two Indians with him had vanished back into the forest. He wandered into the few tents toward the cooking fire. A small group of men stood around it, where an iron pot stood steaming. DiPaolo, baffled, could think of no words. He joined the circle and put down his bag with relief. Suddenly he felt exhausted and hungry.

Finally one of the men glanced at him. It was the commander, Rondon. He said, "Ah. I see you're back. We were afraid we had lost you. Come and sit down."

DiPaolo said, "You have been here all this time? Waiting for me?"

Rondon laughed. "Hardly. We only arrived yesterday. There's a hut over there near the bank. It belongs to a rubber hunter. He has several rubber trees. He has been kind enough to provide us with some grain. We will be pushing on tomorrow. I have purchased one of his boats, and we have two canoes nearly finished."

"But why did it take you so long to get this far?" He paused while someone handed him a tin bowl of gruel and a spoon. It was cooked with some kind of fish. DiPaolo inhaled the smell and found it delicious. He said, "I have been gone for weeks, Tiago and I. Maybe months."

Again Rondon gave a quick laugh. "You're dreaming, Martino. This jungle plays strange tricks with the mind. You have been missing for only three or four days. That's bad enough,but not nowhere near that long. Where is Tiago, by the way?"

DiPaolo without thinking said, "At an Indian village. Friendly Indians. He said he wanted to stay awhile."

Rondon shrugged. "Can't blame him for that. When he decides to return home he will have some wages coming. I shall put them aside. Now get some rest, you can tell us all about it tomorrow on the trek."

DiPaolo was too busy eating to speak or think. He looked around, saw the primitive hut and sheds near the embankment. A rubber plantation. Henry Ford's Model T had created a vast new market for rubber. Now the tree hunters had replaced the old time gold prospectors. There were some who might look around and see little change, but others perceived a vast new world ahead. DiPaolo finished his bowl, slumped to the ground, and fell asleep.

Next morning DiPaolo felt better, yet bewildered. Most of the other men in the party were still weary, half starved, and sick. There were more rapids ahead of them. At least now they had food, either gathered or bought from the rubber men. But they still had miles yet to go and an uncertain future. DiPaolo expected to be questioned about his long absence, yet there seemed to be a lack of curiosity. Probably men were just too tired to care, or to wonder. DiPaolo shouldered his burden with the others and moved on, dragging their canoes and packs through the portage.

Roosevelt was ill, at times feverish and semi conscious. Kermit and another man carried him in a hammock. DiPaolo tried talking to him during a rest break. At first the former president seemed half delirious, but then rallied. He put on his pince nez glasses and peered up at DiPaolo. "Ah. Martino. You're the man who saved my life in Cincinnati."

DiPaolo smiled. "If you say so, sir. But it was your speech that saved your life." DiPaolo would never forget that night. They were on their way to the city auditorium where Roosevelt was to address the crowd. DiPaolo reminded him of the fifty page speech he had written earlier, then nearly forgotten. Roosevelt took it from DiPaolo and stuffed it into his breast pocket, where a few minutes later it stopped a bullet. The Colonel swore DiPaolo had saved his life. Today DiPaolo wished there was something else he might do to save the man.

He said, "What will you do when you get back, sir? Run for office again?"

Roosevelt gave a short laugh and coughed. "Perhaps I may find a war to join. That would be safer than Brazil. I remember now, it was I who invited you on this adventure. You will have quite a story when you get back, no?" He closed his eyes. DiPaolo came away wondering how much longer the Colonel could last. Kermit was nearby and bent to bathe Roosevelt's brow.

"Ah, DiPaolo." The voice came from behind. He turned to see the expedition commander, Rondon. Rondon said, "Do you think your friend Tiago will really remain with the Indians? Won't he get bored?"

DiPaolo smiled. "No telling, sir. I think he may have found a wife. Some of the native girls are lovely."

Rondon nodded toward Roosevelt. "Your president is in a bad way. The doctor operated on his leg to drain the infection. He had to perform surgery on the river bank. Kermit tries to care for his father, but the Colonel needs a hospital. I would not give much for his chances."

DiPaolo could think of nothing to say to that. But he wanted to ask something else. In the short time he had been in camp, the memory of the past month or so had begun to fade, as if a dream. He was not sure how much was real. He asked Rondon, "Sir. Have you ever heard about an ancient city here in the forest? One that still exists?"

Rondon shook his head but did not laugh. "Oh, there are stories to be sure. The City of Gold, they call it. All nonsense, of course. Old legends. I have heard about some explorer who means to mount an expedition to go and look for it. I should not be surprised if he never comes back."

DiPaolo looked around at the surrounding trees that went on forever. "I'm told this forest is the size of India. I think anything could be there, hiding. But I suppose you're right. If there was ever a city, it's swallowed up forever."

By nightfall that evening DiPaolo had almost convinced himself that his stay at the city was indeed a dream. He could remember drinking the strange tea that sent him to other worlds, to the beautiful places that change not. Perhaps his entire months-long stay at the city had been a tea dream. He looked at the river and remembered its name—the River of Doubt. Doubtful waters. He had begun to doubt his memory, his mind, the difference between the dream and the real.

Then he felt the hard object beneath his shirt. He had nearly forgotten it. He pulled it forth to examine. For some reason he had not thought to show it to anyone else. He had not thought of it at all. Now he studied the strange writing and engraved patterns. Perhaps when he returned to civilization he would have it examined by experts. For now, he tucked it back into his shirt. It would not do to show so much gold in public.

Zharov

Jack Harrow tried to see every man leaving the ship. He had surmised that Kwanyin Luk was traveling in disguise, if indeed he was aboard. It even occurred to him that Kwanyin might have booked a passage as a red herring, then either remained in London or taken a different vessel. That would be in character, the sly bastard. But Harrow had to assume he was now back in the States.

There were a few foreigners among the other passengers, but Harrow saw no Chinese. There were several East Indians as well as Europeans - Germans, Italians, French. But most were Americans or Brits. This was not one of the more exclusive luxury transports, not like the recently lost Titanic or her class. The passengers here were not of the ultra rich, nor were they impoverished immigrants. Harrow guessed Kwanyin would choose a ship like this one so as not to stand out. The only passenger that attracted any notice was the Russian. Harrow had learned the man's name, but never got close to him. He was pointed out on deck. The man had a flowing mustache and beard, wore a patch over one eye, and walked with a swagger. A piratical sort, but with expensive silken clothes in the Slavic style. A flowing blouse and high boots. Kwanyin would never choose such an attention-getting disguise.

Harrow decided he was getting nowhere and left the ship, heading for a cheap hotel room. He wasn't sure of his next move. But that afternoon he sent Bernardi a brief wire: *Arrived NY. Believe subject now loose in USA.*

KWANYIN QUICKLY ABANDONED his Russian persona. He went to a locker room at Grand Central Station, where he changed into American clothes, dumping the costume along with most of his luggage. There was one place he wanted to visit in the city while he was there. That was the mailing address where many of his di Paolo Estate donations were sent. The address was a mail drop, apparently a storefront for a small stationery store. Any mail arriving here went to a private box, assigned by name rather than number. Kwanyin's local delegate would come here once a week to empty the box and count the take. Kwanyin wanted to find out if the man was skimming.

He showed his credentials, opened the box, and quickly counted receipts for the past several days. This game was doing well. The amount came to several thousand. Kwanyin made a log of everything in the box including dates. Later he would compare with the agent's detailed accounts. A little skimming was only to be expected. Too much might lead to serious consequences. But Kwanyin would have to wait for his return to London to see the report.

He dined at a modest restaurant, making sure not to be seen in New York's Chinatown. The tong there still held grudges against him. Next morning he boarded a train for San Francisco.

In Chicago there was a layover of several hours to change trains. Kwanyin found a news stand featuring papers from all over the country. In the Washington Post he noticed a brief notice about Roosevelt. The headline read ROOSEVELT EXPEDITION OVERDUE. The gist was simply that it had not yet been heard from. It should have emerged from the forest weeks earlier. Concerns were raised, etc. Etc. Kwanyin didn't bother buying the paper. He did not believe DiPaolo was in Brazil, but this report would buy time for the man to remain out of sight. DiPaolo was meddling in Kwanyin's business. He was sure of it.

He boarded his westbound train that afternoon, paying for a private compartment. He could afford it. Kwanyin smiled. DiPaolo might think he could cause him trouble, but Kwanyin would soon be making millions. Finally he was getting what he deserved.

HARROW REMAINED IN New York for a few days. He knew the Hip Sing Tong here was still looking for Kwanyin. For once they were cooperating with the police. Harrow had his own contacts and got to talk to a man in Chinatown. No, they had heard nothing. Kwanyin had not been seen there. Kwanyin had debts to be paid. He would not be allowed back until they were.

Next, Harrow went to the address he had collected from the "donors." This was the place to where they sent their bank drafts, care of Sr. Pascual. He was a little surprised to find a stationery store; he had expected some sort of office building. The lady behind the counter was well dressed and polite. "May I help you, sir?"

"I am looking for Mr. Pascual. I was told he has an office here."

She smiled. "I'm afraid you are mistaken, sir. There are no offices. I know the name, however. We receive mail for him nearly every day. Did you wish to rent a box?"

Harrow understood. Anyone coming here with a warrant would find only a mailbox. He produced his detective's badge. "How often does Mr. Pascual pick up his mail?"

She held her polite smile. "Never, I'm afraid. Not in person. He has other agents authorized to use the box. They are here two or three times a week. Mr. Pascual does quite a lot of business. I think it is some sort of mail order company."

"I see. Would you have an address where I can reach Mr. Pascual?"

"I do, but I'm not sure he wants it given out. Is he in some sort of trouble, sir?"

"Not at all. It's just a routine investigation for a lawsuit. Mr. Pascual might prove to be a valuable witness. Or perhaps not." He smiled in his turn.

"Well. I suppose it's all right. Just a moment." She opened a card file, searched a moment, then wrote an address on a note paper. She handed it across. "As you can see, it's in London."

One of Harrow's local contacts from his days on the New York police force was a reporter for the *New York Gazette*. Harrow went to see him. Ely McMoran was at his desk, pounding out a story by the hunt and peck method. He looked up, blinking out of a round, wine-stained face. Ely usually stayed sober while working, but not always. Harrow felt relief at finding the man not slurring his words. Ely said, "Jack Harrow. Haven't seen you in years. What brings you to our fair city?"

Harrow sat down. "Working a case, what else? How are you today, Ely?"

Ely pulled out a rag and mopped his brow. "I've been better. Went to the boxing match last night. I should know better by now than mix beer and bourbon."

Harrow couldn't help a laugh. "I guess that gets the job done alright. You working on any big stories right now?"

Ely gave a half sneer. "Not much. I have to make up half what I write. The editors don't mind, long as it sells paper. We're still trying to milk the Titanic for all she's worth. There's going to be hearings and trials and such."

"A sad story." Harrow looked past Ely's shoulder at the bustling city room. The *Gazette* was nowhere in the same league as the *Times* or the *Wall Street Journal,* but it had a fair local circulation. This city had a lot of newspapers. *Gazette* was holding its own. Harrow said, "Heard anything new about the Roosevelt party? Have they turned up in Brazil yet?"

Ely shook his head. "Not so as I know. You interested?"

Harrow said, "My boss is in that expedition." Then he changed the subject. "Want a new story?"

Ely folded his hands on his blotter. "What you got?"

"It's this di Paolo Estate thing. You've heard of that?"

"Who hasn't? I was thinking of investing summat myself."

"Don't. It's a con. A bubble." Then he went on to tell Ely most of what he knew. He left out only his own committing of forgery and fraud, in order to steal from the thief. Ely took notes. When they were done, Ely gave Harrow a wink. "This will be on page one tomorrow. I guarantee it."

And Harrow thought, That is going to rattle Kwanyin's cage.

KWANYIN, ON LEAVING New York, had discarded his Russian costume and accent. However he decided to continue using the name Anton Zharov. He already had papers identifying him as such. Besides, there were still high class hotels and restaurants that would not serve Chinese. Kwanyin could still pass as Slavic, with a British accent. A distant relative of the Romanoffs. It amused him.

The railroads were running well, but it yet took nearly as much time to reach San Francisco as it had to cross the Atlantic. When he finally landed, he went to see O'Shea. O'Shea had been expecting him.

"How was the trip?"

Kwanyin shrugged. "The usual. On the train I was able to sell a couple shares. They paid cash. But I'm no tourist. Bad weather held us up crossing the Rockies."

O'Shea pulled open a desk drawer. "Business has been good. You can see the books any time you're ready. I thought you might want to look at this." He opened an envelope containing several newspaper clippings. He handed the first to Kwanyin. "That's from the New York Gazette, last week. I don't know if you heard about it."

"I didn't get many papers on the train." He spread the clipping. The headline jumped out: DI PAOLO ESTATE A HOAX. In smaller type: *Reveals Private Detective.*

Kwanyin glanced at O'Shea, then read the article. It was a fairly detailed report of how the con worked. It stated flatly the estate did not exist. It concluded: Sr. Pascual claims the estate lawsuit was approved by the "Lords and King Commission." There is no such thing.

Kwanyin looked up, about to say something to O'Shea. But he was holding another clip. "Before you say anything, sir, take a look at this." Kwanyin did. The head ran: **GAZETTE ATTACKED!** *Last night windows of the New York Gazette were smashed by rocks thrown by supporters of the di Paolo estate scheme ...*

Kwanyin read the item through and then burst out laughing. New York by now had its own share of "investors" or "donors" if you prefer. They refused to believe the con was a hoax. They had tried to burn down the newspaper office. Kwanyin said, "This might bring in even more customers."

"Yes sir. There was no way I could reach you, so I took a liberty. I had this run in the Gazette and several other papers." **PASCUAL CONDEMNS HOAX REPORT**. This item was a sworn testimony by the estate executor, to the effect that the estate was real. All necessary documents will be made public in due course. A legal decision was expected in the next ninety days, the estate was worth billions, etc.

Kwanyin looked up from the clip and smiled. "Excellent work, Mr. O'Shea. I am giving you a raise."

O'Shea lit up a cigar. "Yeah, I know."

Civilization

In the next few days, the expedition's state improved somewhat. Rondon was able to deal with some rubber tappers to trade the dugouts for better, lightweight boats that could handle the rapids. There was more food. Then they came to a broken-down river trading post with old inventory and nearly empty shelves. The men gorged themselves. Some drank entire cans of condensed milk. After months of near starvation, they made themselves sick. But they survived, and pushed on.

Roosevelt still ate but little. He was able to keep down a few freshly laid eggs. DiPaolo was horrified to see his condition. The man had lost fifty pounds of his former weight. DiPaolo spent as much time as he could with him, giving Kermit a break. He knew Kermit was afraid the Colonel might not survive this journey. The party of exploration had been out of contact with civilization for more than four months. They had left the last telegraph station in January. It was now late April. In spite of help they found along the way, the men were all exhausted and ill. They knew they would not last much longer. Then they found what they needed.

Near the headwaters of another rapid they came across a large store. Rondon went ahead to parlay with the owner. He came back a short time later. He called the men together and offered a smile.

"This store belongs to a *patroa*. He's a boss. The rubber tappers bring him rubber to exchange for goods. He sells the rubber down river and makes a fortune. He says he will help us free of charge. He will guide us through the rapids."

A murmur ran through the party, in Brazilian and English. DiPaolo sat stunned. This sounded too good to be true. It meant they were nearly home. Almost down river. But a few minutes later Kermit spoke to him in low tones. "Even if we get past these rapids, with food and medicine, that doesn't mean we're out. We will still have miles yet to travel. I can only pray our chances have improved." He turned away to see to his father, then turned back for a moment. "I still can't believe how well you look, how well you came from the jungle. The quinine must have done its work. I wish we could all have found this Indian village of yours." He turned away again.

DiPaolo got the feeling that Kermit thought he was lying about something. He thought of telling him of the herbs the Indians had given him, then decided to remain silent. Kermit would probably choose not to believe him. DiPaolo reminded himself he had not lied. He had merely used the word *village* instead of *city*. In fact he was no longer himself sure of the truth.

Next morning, equipped with good boats and supplies, they set off down the last rapids. They finally had left behind their crude dugout canoe. The patroa of this store took the lead boat. He knew the river and guided them well. They shot the rapids without disaster. The only loss was Kermit's dog, that chose to wander off into the jungle and not return. They came to a waterfall and set off on portage. After a day and a half since leaving the store, they found civilization.

They were walking through a swamp. Rising waters had drowned what islands remained. Overhanging trees cast what seemed a vast pall. After the party's hopes of the day before, a sense of gloom seemed ready to descend. And then they came from shadows into light. Rondon, leading, came to a sudden halt. He held a hand over his head and shouted, <u>Meu deus!</u>

Ahead, on the river embankment, lay an orderly row of tents. DiPaolo turned to Kermit, who stared ahead. Kermit said, "It's

Lieutenant Pyrineus. The relief party. They were supposed to meet us here six weeks ago. They must have been waiting all this time."

Roosevelt turned to DiPaolo. "Say, did I promise you an adventure, Martino? Or was it a vacation, I don't recall? Did you have one of those?"

DiPaolo, dizzy with relief, shook his head. "I believe it was an adventure, Colonel."

After that, the men returned to their various lives. Roosevelt got treatment at a hospital and began a slow recovery. The thirteen surviving camaradas received their pay, bought new clothes, and posed for pictures. The government of Brazil had decided to rename the Rio de Duvidas the Roosevelt River. DiPaolo telegraphed Benita Bernardi that he was alive, safe, and would soon return. He spent a few days in the hospital himself, but was found free of Malaria symptoms or other disease. With some regret, or mixed feelings, he booked passage to New York. He wondered how Tiago was doing.

IT TOOK A DAY OR TWO for details of the expedition's arrival to reach San Francisco. Then the news made the front pages. Roosevelt had survived and was on his way home. Names of other members of the party were not mentioned, with the exception of Martino DiPaolo, the only San Franciscan. Bernardi had got his telegram the day before. She went to see Jack Harrow.

"He's back," she said, holding out the wire. "He's safe."

Harrow glanced at the paper, knowing of course who she meant. "How do you feel? Relieved?"

"Yes, I guess that's the word. It's so inadequate. I feel like an enormous weight has just lifted from my shoulders. I hadn't even known it was there. Do you think I should arrange a homecoming party?"

He opened both hands, making a helpless gesture. "We don't know if he'll feel like a party. Perhaps something quieter, a few friends for supper."

"Yes, I think so. You must come, of course. You can help me plan."

"And I will be happy not to have to run the office anymore. Not that you can't do without me. But I'd rather be out there tracking down Kwanyin or some other evil doer."

She smiled. "I wonder what Martino will say about all that money we stole from the evil doer?"

"We didn't steal it, the evil doer did. We just helped him spend it. Probably still driving him crazy."

"I wonder if he really is crazy. For a crazy man he makes a lot of cash."

Harrow picked up a clipping from his desk, the one about the *New York Gazette* and its broken windows . "I wonder who is the crazy? Kwanyin or his marks?"

DIPAOLO RETURNED ON the same ship as the Colonel and his son Kermit, along with a few others. The doctors had wanted to keep Roosevelt in the hospital longer, but he would have none of that. The old bull moose was showing his head again. He was eating and even taking short walks on deck with the aid of a cane. DiPaolo had many chances to talk to him. He often passed them up except for small talk. He found he could not think of what to say. But on one blustery morning he found the Colonel alone on a deck chair, watching the sea. On impulse he sat beside him. He asked, "Where is Kermit, Colonel? He's not with you today? I hope he's well?"

"Hah! Kermit fusses around me like a mother. I told him to take some time off. Go to the saloon, have a drink, play cards. But leave me be a few hours. Do you think we shall see any whales on this trip?"

"I should like to, sir. I have never seen one."

"Spend any time at sea, you shall. Tell me, Martino, are you happy you made this expedition? It was a hard one."

DiPaolo realized that if Roosevelt admitted it was hard even for him, then it must indeed have been hard. He said in answer, "I had experiences I never dreamed of, sir. I should not care to do it again. But I think they changed me. For better or worse, I could not yet say."

"I believe I understand you." He turned to look DiPaolo in the face. "Sometimes a man changes without knowing it. Now and then, perhaps only once or twice in a lifetime, a change happens so profound he can't understand it. Perhaps he's not even aware of it until much later. In my lifetime, I have had one or two of those myself. I advise you not to turn your back, Martino." Having said this, Roosevelt turned his own back to the sea.

DiPaolo looked also to the sea. He remembered again the magical tea, that had transported him to a sea of light and understanding, to a different, unchanging world that was both real and unreal. For a moment he soared into the sky.

The Con

Kwanyin Luk also saw those items in the San Francisco papers. The Roosevelt expedition had finally turned up, long overdue. There had been fears for their safety, etc. In fact they had suffered losses and many were ill, including the former president. But now they were safe and headed home, and so on. Some of the papers mentioned Martino DiPaolo, the only San Francisco member. He was said to be in good health, unlike most of the others.

Kwanyin said, "Hah!" He had been reading some of the papers to O'Shea. "They're still pretending DiPaolo was on that expedition. I know he has been here all the time, sabotaging me, stealing from my bank account. He knows I can't prove it. I can't go to the police because I shouldn't be in this country. He's clever, I'll give him that."

O'Shea was looking through some of the other journals. This city had more than a dozen newspapers including weeklies. About half of them were on his desk. He said, "This one is funny. There's not enough news, so they're making things up. I guess they couldn't find DiPaolo for an interview."

"So. What sort of things are they making up?"

O'Shea smiled. "There's this twaddle about lost cities in the jungle. Cities of gold and so on. Seems there's this explorer who wants to and look. He's supposed to be getting an expedition together."

Kwanyin looked up. "Now that gives me an idea. Sooner or later this DiPaolo estate con is going to run its course. It's going to stop paying off. Supposing we were to start an expedition of our own? A search for the Lost City of Gold. We could begin asking for donations.

You might be the archeologist. Go on a lecture tour, present magic lantern shows, or even moving pictures? With a few prominent names enrolled, we could rake in thousands. What do you say?"

O'Shea didn't look impressed. But he gave a shrug and said, "Worth a try, I guess. Meanwhile, this di Paolo con is still paying off. No point in giving up on it yet."

"No, there isn't." Kwanyin fell silent, thinking. He said, "Do you know why I'm back in the States, O'Shea?"

"Sure. To check up on me and your other deputies. To make sure we're not skimming your income."

"That's one reason." In fact he had not given any reason at all to O'Shea before this. He had simply wired that he was coming for a visit. He said, "DiPaolo is too much of a nuisance. I have taken legal steps to prevent him from accessing my bank accounts again. But the fact he did it once can not be tolerated. I have come here to find and kill him."

O'Shea put down the paper he had been glancing over. "That's not in my line, Luk. But I know a few operators who could steer you to the right man."

"No!" Kwanyin shook his head. "No, this has become too personal. I should have done this years ago. I will find the man myself and eliminate him. From you, I may need a hideout and a quick exit from town. I was thinking of returning to England by ship, by way of Panama. What do you think?"

O'Shea gave him a serious, long look. "That can be arranged, Mr. Kwanyin. For a price, of course."

"Of course."

Now he just had to find DiPaolo.

DIPAOLO REMAINED IN New York for several days because the doctors insisted they had to check him for possible diseases from the jungle. He did not object. After the last trip down the River of Doubt and the voyage by ship, he was happy to remain in one place for awhile. He still looked forward to days aboard a train. Benita was able to get through by long distance telephone to his hotel. They spoke for about twenty minutes, and the charge of course was astronomical. The talk was mostly personal, but she took a few minutes to fill him in on Kwanyin and the DiPaolo estate scheme. This was the first he'd heard of it—U.S. news was often late getting to Brazil. She summed it up with, "Don't worry, Martino. I'll fill you in when you get here. You will never believe what Harrow pulled off. I won't tell you on the phone, but I think you will be pleased. Oh, and Martino?"

"Yes?"

"I love you." She clicked off.

The doctors all said they were amazed at DiPaolo's health. Most of the other expedition party were still suffering from after effects of malnutrition, scurvy, or fever. There was yellow fever, malaria, and two or three diseases they didn't know about. One man had lost a thumb by trailing his hand in piranha infested water.

In due course DiPaolo got his all clear. He had not much to pack. He had lost most of his belongings in Brazil, and had to buy clothes in New York. He packed everything into one suitcase. One of the doctors who examined him had remarked on the gold medal he wore beneath his shirt. DiPaolo glanced at it with surprise. He had forgotten he still had it on. He said, "Oh, that. A good luck charm. An Indian gave it to me. Not real gold, of course."

He spent much of his time on the train sleeping.

KWANYIN LUK WAS GETTING frustrated. He had expected to be in San Francisco not more than a few days. Now he had been here already two weeks. That did give him a chance to monitor more closely the work of his deputies around the country. Many of them worked for free, convinced they would be getting rich by buying and selling shares in the estate. Others accepted payment in the form of fifty dollar shares. A few, like O'Shea, were in on the con. They had to be paid in cash, and watched to make sure they didn't steal too much.

But that was not why Kwanyin was here. He had expected to find DiPaolo either hiding out at home, or at his detective agency. DiPaolo was hunting Kwanyin. He thought he was being clever by his pretense of being out of the country. Kwanyin was more clever still. He was hunting the hunter.

He remembered what he had read and studied of <u>The Art of War</u> by Sun Tzu. This war master had discussed the need for spies. There were several different kinds of spies, according to Sun Tzu. There was what he called the "external spy." This was one who remained outside the enemy camp looking in. The "internal spy," on the other hand, was imbedded with the enemy and reporting out. That was who Kwanyin needed. A spy in DiPaolo's office. He went to see O'Shea.

"I have a job opening. I want to put a spy in DiPaolo's business."

O'Shea picked up a new cigar and sniffed it. "Anyone in mind?"

"Yes. Your secretary. Miss Gwen."

Her real name was Gwendolyn Jones. She did not care to use such a common last name, and so let people call her Miss Gwen, or just Gwen depending on how they knew each other. She had never been arrested and was not exactly a criminal herself, but she made a good living by being useful to criminals. She knew how to keep her mouth shut. She was even a good member of her church.

Early Monday morning she presented herself at the DiPaolo Detective Agency. She introduced herself as Mrs. Jones.

"How can I help you, Mrs. Jones?" The man at the front desk asked. There were only four male detectives and one woman. They took turns at the front.

She adjusted her skirt. "I am having a problem with my ex husband. A most serious problem. Is Mr. DiPaolo in? I was told to ask for him."

"Mr. DiPaolo is not yet back from New York. We expect him by the end of the week, but I'm not sure when he will return to the office. Mr. Harrow is in charge at present."

"I see. May I speak to Mr. Harrow then?"

She waited patiently while Harrow interviewed another client. She declined all offers to speak to anyone else. She also declined coffee or tea. Eventually she was let in to Harrow's office. She explained her problem. "My husband, Oliver Jones. Here is a photograph." She pushed a photo across Harrow's desk. It was of a well dressed, overweight man with sideburns and beard. He was seated, holding a walking stick. O'Shea had provided the picture from somewhere. He had no idea who the man actually was.

"Mr. Jones, you see, is quite wealthy, in the oil business. There is a court order that he pay me a certain monthly amount of alimony. He is now three months delinquent. He is claiming bankruptcy, but I have information he has just purchased a yacht and has a new mistress. I have reason to suspect he has been embezzling from his firm."

Harrow nodded. "And of course you will need proof to take him to court. I think we can help you, Mrs. Jones. But we will need more information to track down your spouse. I'm going to assign one of our detectives to take all necessary details. He will explain to you our usual rates."

"I shall be happy to provide details." O'Shea and Kwanyin had worked up an elaborate story to feed the agents. She added, "However, I should like to speak to Mr. DiPaolo personally. If he is your boss, I want to see him before committing myself."

"I'm sure that can be arranged, as soon as he returns."

"Very well. I shall provide all details about Oliver immediately. But I must insist on seeing Mr. DiPaolo as soon as he shall return."

Harrow smiled. "I'm sure he will be happy to see you. Please leave your number if you have a telephone. I will let you know." He handed her off to one of the agents who happened to be in the office, then returned to his desk. He shrugged. You met all kinds in this business. But he had a strange feeling he had seen Mrs. Jones somewhere before.

Home

As it happened, it was next day when Benita Bernardi received the wire from DiPaolo. He was at last boarding the train home. He sent her his anticipated time of arrival in Oakland. When she read the message Benita felt a weight drop from her shoulders, one she hadn't known was there. For months she had been telling herself and others there was nothing to fear, that Martino was safe and would soon return. And yet she had feared, with a deeply buried terror of never seeing him again, with never a chance to say farewell.

Yes, she planned to celebrate quietly. She would arrange a special supper in his honor, inviting Jack Harrow and perhaps all the others in his agency. A few of her own friends in the police department. One or two others she might think of later. But not a noisy celebration with music or dancing. A quiet, unspoken ritual of thanksgiving. Reading Martino's message again, she felt she ought to laugh and sing. Instead, she fell to her knees and sobbed with relief.

Next morning, she took a street car to the agency. She shared the telegram with Harrow and the others. Harrow asked if she knew when DiPaolo would return to the office.

"He didn't say, Jack. I suppose he might want a few days to rest and get his bearings. Are you ready to give up being a boss?"

"Ready as rain. I'm happier when I'm out in the streets, knocking on doors and bothering people. By the way, it happens there's someone here who also wants to see him. A client. She's been coming by every day to find out when Martino is going to show up. I'm not sure why."

"Who would that be?"

Harrow looked out his office door toward a well dressed lady sitting in the waiting room. "Her name is Jones. Trying to find a run-off husband. She paid the fifty dollar advance fee, but she hasn't been too helpful. I assigned Danny over there. He says she hasn't given him many clues about how to locate her Oliver. She wants to see Martino."

"I'll go talk to her." Bernardi crossed the office to where the lady waited, and introduced herself. She said, "I understand you wish to locate your spouse, Mrs. Jones."

"I do. I try to come by now and then to see if there has been any progress. I especially want to see Mr. DiPaolo. I was told he is the only one who can help me."

"I understand." Bernardi decided that this lady, respectable and prosperous looking, might be somewhat distracted in her mind. She said, "You may certainly see Mr. DiPaolo when he returns, but I can't say exactly when that will be. In the meantime ..."

"You say you don't know when he will return? Is there any news at all?"

"As a matter of fact, yes. I just learned his train is due in on Monday. But I don't know when he will be able to return to the office. We won't know until we see him."

"Monday, you say. I am so glad to hear this. Perhaps Mr. DiPaolo would be good enough to allow me an interview at his home?"

"Again, I can't say. If you can give me your card, I shall certainly ask him when I see him."

"You are so kind." Mrs. Jones dug an embossed card from her bag and passed it over. Kwanyin had ordered the cards just for this.

"In the meantime, I'd suggest you remain at home, there's not much point in coming here every day. I promise I will call at once when Mr. DiPaolo is at hand."

"Yes." She stood up. "Yes, I suppose you are correct. It's just that I'm so anxious, you see. I shall remain at home and try to be patient, Miss Bernardi." She turned to go. Bernardi watched her leave, glad to be rid of her. No doubt she was an innocent victim, but Bernardi found her annoying. She returned to Harrow to talk about a welcome dinner.

GWEN JONES DID NOT go home. She went directly to O'Shea's office, where Kwanyin had relocated from his hotel. That was not to save money—he wanted to be close to O'Shea's telephone and other contacts. O'Shea was out but Kwanyin was in the office, going through the list of his current deputies and the weekly take. Jones told him what she had heard.

Kwanyin glanced at the clock. Today was Friday. He said, "Thank you, Miss Gwen. Monday morning, then. All trains from the east terminate in Oakland. It shouldn't be hard to find him. You have done well. Here's a small bonus for you." He pushed a gold coin across the desk.

"Thank you, sir. Shall I be needed again to watch the DiPaolo agency?"

"I think not, but I'll keep you in mind. You have proven yourself useful, Miss Gwen. I may have other jobs for you."

She picked up the coin, slipped it into her bag and left without another word. Miss Gwen knew when to keep her mouth shut. Kwanyin got on the telephone and began checking train schedules. He patted the gun in his pocket, which he now carried at all times.

MARTINO DIPAOLO HAD spent days looking out the window of his train compartment, watching the American landscape slide by in silence except for the rhythmic click of rails. He had a sense that he was looking at something not quite real. It was like watching one of those moving pictures, except in color. And seemingly without an end in sight. He had an idea to write down his memories of the Rio de Duvidas expedition. Or the Roosevelt River trip, as it was now called.

He wrote in the form of short notes and disconnected sentences: *snakes, poison frogs, insects, spiders, no safe place.* He found it difficult to organize his thoughts. Nevertheless, he was able to trace an outline of his memories, until he got to the part about the city. He had been there either months, or a few days. Did it really exist, or was it all his fevered mind? What had really happened to Tiago? He tried to write something about the experience and found he could not.

DiPaolo did attempt to strike up conversations with a few men in the lounge car. Most of their talk was of trivial matters - sports or politics. But one of them reacted when DiPaolo told him his name. "You're a DiPaolo, then? One of the DiPaolo heirs?" That was the first time Martino heard about the heir con.

He spoke with another man traveling to California, who seemed to collect newspapers. DiPaolo mentioned the Roosevelt expedition, without revealing that he had been a member. The other man pulled out one of his papers.

"Yes, very interesting. There's a lengthy item about that in the Tribune. It was led by this fellow named Rondon. A strange fellow, it says here. He was head of the Brazil national telegraph project, you see. He saw to stringing hundreds of miles of copper wire through the jungle. It took years, and several hundred men lost their lives to disease or accident or Indian attack. Funny thing is, now the project is complete. But they don't need it anymore. Brazil is taking up the Marconi wireless system. Think of that! Now they can send hundreds of messages through the ether instead of a few at a time on copper wire. So all that work by this Rondon was for nothing."

DiPaolo listened and tried to absorb that news. He found his sense of reality retreating further from his mind.

ON MONDAY MORNING KWANYIN Luk arrived early. There were two trains due to arrive that morning from the east. One got in at seven, the other at almost noon. Kwanyin, in one of his many disguises, was waiting. A great many passengers debarked at seven. The train was only six minutes late. Kwanyin had been there for an hour, watching for any sign of Benita Bernardi. In his railroad porter's uniform, no one noticed him. If anyone glanced in his direction, they saw only a stoop-shouldered Chinese laborer. He carried a broom and dustpan, now and then pausing to pick up litter. He waited patiently. The gun inside his jacket made no bulge.

Bernardi showed up around eleven. She was accompanied by a man Kwanyin recognized as Jack Harrow. The fact that she was here meant one thing to Kwanyin—the story about DiPaolo being out of town was true.But Kwanyin did not believe for a moment he had been in Brazil. Probably he had been in New York or London, meddling in Kwanyin's business. A reckoning was due.

There came a scream of brakes and crash of couplings as the great steam engine slammed to a halt. It was as if the iron beast protested against stopping, it wanted to continue, crashing past the rails and into the station itself. Kwanyin, in the sidelines, waited. Bernardi and her friend also waited, watching passengers emerge from cars, swiveling their heads to inspect each one. After a few minutes they suddenly broke and rushed forward. Kwanyin waited for them to return from the track. He did not wait long. DiPaolo and his two friends came forward, brushing past others standing around or trying to collect baggage. The man Bernardi had come with carried only a small bag. DiPaolo had his arm around Bernardi's waist.

Kwanyin stepped forward, feeling for the butt of his revolver. But he paused. He saw this was not the right place or time. There were railroad police about. Too many witnesses. Much too public. Kwanyin was not stupid. His hatred of this old enemy of his urged him to rush forward and shoot without a word. Take the man down, turn and run. But he knew better. He would have a poor chance of getting away. He would wait. He would draw DiPaolo into a trap, as a spider draws a fly. Kwanyin smiled.

DIPAOLO, HARROW, AND Bernardi took a motor taxi to Bernardi's house. For DiPaolo, the first order of business was a hot bath, after so many days on the train. Bernardi scrubbed his back. Harrow left DiPaolo's luggage, such as it was. Then he left them alone, promising to return for supper. Bernardi, who had not spoken much until DiPaolo had finished his bath, said, "I missed you."

"And I you. Will you marry me, Benita?"

She shrugged. "Sure, why not? I have made worse mistakes. How was your expedition? There are all sorts of reports."

He turned to look at her. He hadn't really expected her to say <u>yes.</u> He wondered even now if she were joking. He said, "The expedition? It was hard. Men died. I had a friend who decided to stay with the Indians. They tell me I was delirious with fever. We were afraid Roosevelt would not survive. But we made it through." He was looking through the closet, trying to find something that fit. The clothes he had been wearing were all donated in Brazil. His own were now all too large. He had a vague memory of getting on a scale back in the hospital, and being shocked. He wasn't sure how much he'd lost. He said, "I think I'd rather talk about that later. Tell me what has been going on here. I heard something about a <u>di Paolo Estate </u>scheme."

"Indeed." She poured two glasses of sherry and handed him one. "Kwanyin Luk is behind that. It began shortly after you left. While the cat's away ... Jack Harrow has been looking into it." She went on to tell DiPaolo everything she knew about the con. DiPaolo smiled.

"He stole all that cash from Kwanyin? That man must be furious. I wondered what had become of him. So he's been in London. I imagine he'll stay there to avoid American authorities. At least till he breaks some British law." He paused, savoring the sherry. He realized he had not touched a drop of alcohol in months. Suddenly it seemed strange, the taste, aroma, and effect. Not unpleasant, but as if he had never tried it before. He shook his head. "What I don't like is my own name being a part of this con. I suppose that's why Luk decided to use it. He knew I'd be angry. Almost like a challenge. Tomorrow I'll go down to the agency and read the files."

She said, "Are you sure you're ready to go back to work?"

"No. In fact, I have been thinking about finding something else to do, I'm not sure what. If you're serious about marriage, maybe you can help me decide. But first I need to do something about Kwanyin."

"I was serious, Martino. Once you get settled, we can take our vows and honeymoon in Hawaii. Or anywhere else you please. Turn your agency over to Harrow. He's a good man."

DiPaolo sipped his sherry, nodded, remained silent. She said, "Tell me about the Indian village where you stayed. You say they gave you that gold medal."

He looked directly at her, staring. He had an urge to explain about the city. Yet he found he could not. He said, "It was just a peaceful little town. That's all."

More Plans

Kwanyin consulted with O'Shea. They both went over the books, comparing notes. The weekly income still looked good, though not as good as it had once been. Kwanyin wondered if it might be time to change the game. O'Shea handed him a clipping from the Oakland Tribune. "Have you seen this yet? It's from yesterday."

Kwanyin scanned the item. It was another expose of the di Paolo estate scheme. These reports seemed to be appearing more often in local papers. So far they seemed to have no real evidence, no testimony of witnesses or court documents. They usually ended with some sort of disclaimer that the reporter had been unable so far to contact the supposed executor, Sr. Pascual. Kwanyin tossed the clipping to the floor. "Actually, that gives me an idea."

"So?" O'Shea did not consider himself a criminal genius. He was no brain. Nor did he have ambitions to lead a gang. He was content to let others with more enterprise lead. O'Shea was just office help. Then, when the fall came, if it did, the man on top would have further to drop. The ones on the bottom might rise to the top. O'Shea would remain in the middle. He leaned back in his office chair and waited for Kwanyin to tell him his idea. There was a background noise of Miss Gwen clacking away on her typewriter. Neither man paid attention.

Kwanyin said, "How much liquid cash do we have in the account right now? Not securities or bonds, just real money?"

O'Shea flipped open his account book, found the correct line, and read off the amount. Kwanyin nodded. "That is a large sum. It doesn't even include what I have stashed in Europe. We can afford to invest some."

"Invest how?"

At this Kwanyin's expression seemed to take on a grin of slight mischief. "The skeptics always complain no investor has yet to receive a dime of their contribution back. Let's change that. Let's make a list of the first five hundred donors on our list. The first investors who bought into our game. Then I'll have Miss Gwen type up a form letter. Something like this: *The Chancery Court has begun to move in our favor, such that we are now able to begin collecting and releasing funds. We are therefore remitting to you under separate cover the first monetary return on your investment. We expect further funds to become rapidly available, and shall release them as quickly as possible. Please look forward to more returns in the next few weeks. Yours sincerely, etc.*

Kwanyin looked pleased with himself. "I shall have five hundred copies printed, each individually signed by Sr. Pascual. After the letters have been mailed, we shall send bank drafts, under registered mail, to each of the five hundred recipients. In the amount of one thousand dollars each."

O'Shea let out a breath. "That will cost us five hundred thousand dollars."

Kwanyin laughed. "It won't cost us a dime. We will see to it this makes every paper in the country. Especially the Oakland Tribune. I'll bet you we get a million dollars in new donations by the next week."

At that, O'Shea shook his head. "Mr. Kwanyin, you are a genius."

Miss Gwen, unsummoned, came into the office with a notepad. "You wished to dictate a letter, sir?"

That was only the first part of Kwanyin's plan. He had not forgotten Martino DiPaolo or Benita Bernardi. But he was biding his time. The form letters went out in the mail, some to addresses in California, others to places further east. O'Shea made sure to notify all of their agents of the impending payments. He sent the names of those about to receive them. News stories were planted in many papers. Many of those papers chose to ignore the tips, but others, short on copy, ran items on pages one or two—*First Payoffs to di Paolo Estate.*

Then, when he was ready, Kwanyin placed a quarter page advert in both the *Examiner* and the *Tribune.* It read,

Sr. Pascual announces seminar on di Paolo estate.

The copy described an upcoming seminar on the current legal status of the di Paolo lawsuits. The purpose was to reassure investors their funds were safe, and how best to make free donations to this noble cause. Especially intended for new donors. It was important not to call them "investors." Investments were taxable, donations were not. The advert concluded: Date And Time to be Announced. Always keep the marks dangling on a string, a basic principal of the good con. Kwanyin settled back to wait. He wanted to see what DiPaolo would do.

DIPAOLO WAS SPENDING some time at his office, reading files. He wanted to get up to speed on Kwanyin's schemes. Yet somehow, he felt a sense of detachment. He had been trying to pin this man down for years. For a time he had disappeared from view. DiPaolo should have felt excited now that his enemy was nearly in sight. Yet somehow he felt apart, as though the problem had become less important. DiPaolo had moments when he asked himself what indeed had importance? Benita was important. Sometimes he remembered the City of Gold, then at others he wondered if that had been some sort of fever dream. How long had he spent there, anyway? He wished he could return again, to see Tiago and the city. Then he wondered if it really existed.

He tried to concentrate on the problem of Kwanyin. When he realized how much money the man was raking in he felt shocked and amazed. Again, he began to question the nature of reality. All that cash had no basis of existence. It was founded on lies and dreams. And yet, thousands believed in it. As long as people believed in the money, it was real. Otherwise, it was nothing but numbers in books.

Jack Harrow said one day, "I remember now where I met Mrs. Jones. She was working for that O'Shea character. He called her Miss Gwen."

"Ha. The woman has talent." DiPaolo grinned. She would make a good female agent, if she wanted to go straight. But I suppose it wouldn't pay as well."

"What do you want to do about O'Shea? We could nail him now for mail fraud. Just call in the Postal boys."

"Not yet. He's not the biggest fish. Let me know if you dig up anything new."

"Matter of fact, there is." Harrow had just come into the office. He unfolded a copy of that afternoon's *Examiner*. He showed DiPaolo the notice about the upcoming seminar. DiPaolo smiled.

"I think we must both register to attend, don't you?"

That evening, DiPaolo had a quiet evening dining with Benita. She had begun cooking some meals by herself, giving her cook the night off. She was discovering she enjoyed it, as long as it wasn't every day. This evening she served a poached sea bass, with a custard dessert. She said, "I began cooking more often while you were away. It didn't make sense to hire a cook just to make my light meals. Half the time I ate out anyway."

He said between mouthfuls, "It's delicious." He was still remembering the welcome home supper. Benita had prepared some of that herself. There had been only a few guests, including Harrow and three men she knew from the police, with their wives. He said, "I was surprised at some of those questions the coppers asked. I didn't know they were so interested in Brazil, or knew as much as they did."

She smiled. "You didn't see all the newspaper and magazine articles. There were hundreds of stories about the jungle, the Indians and wild animals. Especially after you lost contact. *Will Roosevelt return? Is the expedition lost?* Some of their descriptions of the jungle were far fetched."

"Maybe not as far fetched as the reality. Do you know there are two hundred pound catfish down there? Their mouths are so big they don't need to bite, just swallow their prey whole. And there are ants an inch long . . ." He trailed off, remembering.

She said, "I admit to reading a couple of books about it myself. Did you know there was a Spanish explorer on the Amazon years before the conquistadors or colonists? He reported there were cities and villages all along the river, with farmland and trading posts. He said they had fine ceramics, gold, and artwork, a high civilization. But then, when the next explorers showed up a few years later they found nothing but jungle. They had to conclude the first man there was lying."

DiPaolo shook his head. "He wasn't lying."

"How do you know he wasn't?"

He started to answer, but then found his throat begin to choke. He said, "Just a feeling."

A week later an announcement arrived in the mail, a letter addressed to Benita Bernardi. Since she had donated one hundred dollars to the di Paolo estate project, her name was on the mailing list. The letter was an invitation to the first seminar session for registered donors. This was to be exclusive for previous donors. There would be a later session open to the general public, date to be announced. Benita showed the letter to DiPaolo when he got home. He read it twice. "Would you like to go?"

She laughed. "Of course."

"It says here you can bring a guest. I'm your guest."

"You're on."

Trap

The seminar was held in a public hall in the Mission District. Not the most elegant location, but it was easy to get to. It drew a large crowd. Kwanyin Luk kept his distance, watching from the wings. The backstage was cluttered with apparatus from some earlier theater production, a fake wagon, cotton clouds, several rolled up backdrops. Kwanyin took his seat on something that looked like a bale of hay, but was hollow inside and weighed almost nothing. He wore a new disguise - padding to make him look fat, a grey beard and mustache. If anyone asked, he was one of Pascual's lawyers.

Pascual himself was represented by a professional actor hired by O'Shea. That man was a real resource when it came to finding talent. Kwanyin kept his eyes on the crowd filing in to the auditorium. Admission was by invitation only. If someone had forgotten to bring the letter, his name was checked on a list. They entered one at a time. Martino DiPaolo and Benita Bernardi were among the first to arrive. O'Shea had thoughtfully provided a piano player to play soft background music while the crowd got settled. Kwanyin's target was in the third row from the front.

He thought it over. O'Shea of course did not know Kwanyin's real plan. Kwanyin hoped to lure DiPaolo backstage after the presentation. It would be easy to think of a pretext - Pascual might want to give him him secret information unknown to the public. Once Kwanyin got DiPaolo away from the crowd, he would simply shoot him. Nothing fancy, just step from behind a screen and kill. It would be over fast. Kwanyin had his escape route planned. Drop the disguise, disappear into Chinatown. The day after tomorrow, he had a cabin reserved on a ship bound for Panama. He had not told O'Shea or anyone else about this. O'Shea might have to take the fall. That was all right, as long as Kwanyin could still access the bank accounts. It was past time to shut down the di Paolo estate con.

Kwanyin did not know that Jack Harrow was also in the audience. Harrow did not have an invitation, but he had the name of one of the invitees. It was a man Harrow had interviewed and managed to convince he had been swindled. That in itself was not easy. Harrow had read some of Mark Twain. He remembered Twain's remark that it's easier to cheat a man than it is to convince him he has been cheated. Harrow used this particular man's name, William Grady. It was on the list. Harrow took a seat near the rear of the hall.

The pianist was playing Viennese waltzes on an upright. The presentation was supposed to start at eight. It was nearly a quarter after before the crowed started getting restless. Harrow guessed there were about two hundred in the audience. O'Shea had not sent that many invitations out, but people were encouraged to bring guests. Give them an opportunity to invest. Everyone can get rich. The music died away at O'Shea's signal, and he took center stage. The place had good acoustics, and his voice carried.

"Friends, neighbors, investors!" O'Shea held up a hand for silence. "Welcome! I know you all have questions, which we will try to answer. There have been a lot of rumors and false accusations going around. I hope this evening will conquer any doubts that anyone might have been harboring. After the presentation, we'll answer any and all questions you may have. But first, a surprise! One of the vile rumors that's been going around is about Signor J.T. Pascual, the di Paolo estate's executor. One of the false accusations put out there is that he does not even exist! Of course Signor Pascual makes few public appearances in view of his legal responsibilities. However, we have arranged for him to address you all tonight, face to face. There will be time for questions afterward. I therefore bring to you, straight from London—the honorable Signor J.T. Pascual!"

At that, O'Shea stepped aside, raising his hands to clap. Pascual himself stepped out from the wings, bowing. The audience erupted in applause. Some got to their feet. Pascual smiled and waved, waiting till the applause died, then stepped to the podium, shuffling a sheaf of notes. He was actually a second generation Italian American who had never been to Europe. He sometimes worked in Vaudeville. O'Shea knew him only as Tony. He had a convincing accent and could speak some Italian if necessary.

The presentation got under way. Pascual/Tony was good. He began by rattling off figures, the amount of capital believed to be in the di Paolo estate, amounts of interest compounded annually, real property included, etc. etc. Lights were dimmed and magic lantern slides projected on a screen. Graphs, charts, lists of numbers. Also photographs of ancient scrolls purported to be the last testament of di Paolo himself, together with other legal documents incomprehensible to anyone.

Forty five minutes into the lecture, Pascual signaled for the lights to come up. There would be a ten minute break. It was then that an usher approached Martino DiPaolo and handed him a slip of paper. It read, *Please come at once. I have vital information for you. Follow the usher. Come alone. Pascual.*

DiPaolo showed the note to Benita, raising an eyebrow. She shrugged. He left the note with her and got up to follow the usher. He was alone. But at the rear of the hall, Jack Harrow saw. He also rose and followed.

On the way down a long, narrow corridor, DiPaolo had time to wonder if this Pascual was real. It was certainly possible. Kwanyin might have heard about this Pascual who was working on an unclaimed estate. Kwanyin might have decided to exploit Pascual, turning the whole case into a gigantic bubble. That could be what Pascual himself wanted to tell him. Then again, DiPaolo was not yet convinced that Pascual actually existed. He could be another part of the con. DiPaolo meant to find out.

Harrow had seen DiPaolo and the usher go through a back door into a darkened hallway. He slipped through a few seconds later, hanging back so that neither would notice. He had told DiPaolo he planned to be in the audience. He had not mentioned he planned to stick like a shadow.

DiPaolo followed the usher to the back of the hall. The corridor had a couple of doors opening off one side, both of them closed. At the end was another door like the others. The usher opened it and stepped back. DiPaolo could see no threat in the man. He was about fifty, thin and frail, wearing a threadbare dark suit. He looked as if he had not been in the sun for a long time. He said, "Mr. Pascual said to wait here. He will be with you in a moment." DiPaolo stepped through the door and it closed behind him. The room looked like it might be a break room for performing theatrical artists. There was a small table, several chairs, a sofa. Electric lamps, a small writing desk.

DiPaolo's hackles went up. There was something wrong here, something missing. Why wasn't Pascual waiting for him? DiPaolo was about to turn and exit by the door he'd come in, when another door on the other side of the room opened. A man DiPaolo recognized came in. DiPaolo said, "Hello, Kwanyin. I thought you were out of town."

Kwanyin had shed his disguise and wore clothing typical of Chinatown—dark green pants and jacket, clean white shoes. A small round cap completed the outfit. In Chinatown he would disappear into the background. He held a revolver in his hand. He said, "I hope you have not too much missed me. I heard the same of you, that you were out of town. Now we are both back where we began."

"We began in San Francisco Bay, when the *Rio* went down. You saved my life. But then you tried to kill me."

Kwanyin paused, breathing deep. Perhaps composing himself. Finally he said, "Enough talk. I am here to finish it." He pulled the trigger. At that range he could not miss. DiPaolo felt something slam into his chest. Then the world went dark.

After that, several things happened almost at once. Kwanyin, seeing DiPaolo's body hit the floor, turned and exited by the way he had come in. Harrow, hearing the shot, burst into the room. He was in time to see Kwanyin disappear into the dark corridor beyond. Instead of giving chase, he bent to DiPaolo's body to check for life signs. Then Benita Bernardi appeared, her face a mask of either rage or fear, Harrow could not tell which. He pointed across the room. He said, "That way!"

In that instant, Benita Bernardi made a choice in contradiction of her most basic instinct to see if her beloved Martino was alive or dead. But Harrow was already doing that. Instead of stopping, her absolute fury took command. She ran across the room after Kwanyin, into the opposite corridor.

Now she was behind him. This hallway was only a few yards long. Kwanyin had stopped at the back door, which was marked EXIT. He was tugging at the door latch with both hands. Apparently it was stuck. Benita screamed. "*You shot my man!*" Then she fired once, low, with her own pistol.

Kwanyin went down, struck in the knee. He gave a shout of pain, then clawed inside his jacket for his gun. Benita kicked him in the head.

Living

Benita Bernardi was talking. DiPaolo could hear, but he had lost track of the conversation. He was still a little dizzy, fading in and out. At least he was becoming more in than out. Bernardi said, "Kwanyin was a fool. He didn't try to draw his weapon until after I had fired. He probably assumed a lady would not carry a gun. He must have forgotten my uncle was a policeman. Most of my best friends are coppers. Why wouldn't I know how to use a gun?"

DiPaolo tried to sit up in bed, but found his chest hurt. He lay back again. "Why am I in hospital? I don't need a doctor."

She leaned over and kissed him on the brow. "We'll be going home. They just wanted to check you. You may have a fracture of your breastbone. They want to do one of those X ray things."

Jack Harrow appeared behind her. "You're the luckiest man alive. Well, one of them. Remember when you saved Roosevelt's life when you handed him his speech? He stuck it in his coat and it stopped a bullet. Kwanyin's would have gone through your heart, except for that fake gold medallion you wear. It *is* fake, isn't it? It could be worth a fortune."

DiPaolo felt for the medallion, but it wasn't there. Benita dipped into her handbag and produced it. She said, "The doctor took it off you. He said the impact over your heart knocked you out, but you should recover. Here's your medal back. Kwanyin's bullet is still embedded in it. I think it's a thirty-eight caliber."

Harrow leaned over for a closer look under the light. "Those are strange inscriptions. I think I've seen something similar in a museum. They look sort of Inca. You say an Indian gave it to you?"

DiPaolo held the medal in his hand a moment. Without answering, he slipped the chain around his neck. His face held a faint smile. He remembered Kerkan's promise that the amulet would protect him from evil.

AFTER THAT, THERE CAME all the fuss and bother. DiPaolo wanted to marry Benita and go on a cruise to Hawaii, but they wouldn't let him leave yet. Criminal investigations require a lot of paperwork and time. One good thing about them was all the publicity for the DiPaolo Detective Agency. At some point DiPaolo announced his decision to resign and turn the company over to Jack Harrow. Harrow had to be talked into it, but finally agreed. DiPaolo said to Benita, "It was fun solving mysteries, as a detective. But now I see this world is full of far greater mysteries. I don't know what I'll do next. Maybe study for a degree. But I won't be satisfied with only the *little* mysteries."

DiPaolo often read the *Morning Call* to Benita. About a month after the shooting, he looked up with a surprised expression. He said, "They're not going to try Kwanyin for attempted murder. Even though he tried to kill me twice."

She turned from looking out the window at San Francisco morning fog and wondering if it was worth going outside today. "Why ever not?"

He tossed the paper aside. "For one thing, the Federals want him for mail fraud. They seem to think that's more important than murder. He could get twenty years at Leavenworth. After he serves his time, the State of California gets him."

"So he gets a long vacation either way."

"Yes, except it looks like he won't go to either trial yet." DiPaolo gave a sudden laugh. "I have to hand it to the man. Kwanyin is the ultimate con artist. According to that item in the paper he's managed to convince a psychiatrist that he's insane. He's being transferred from prison to Napa State Hospital for an indefinite period." He laughed again.

Benita turned from the window. "I don't think that's funny. What if he escapes again?" She turned to look at DiPaolo's medallion where it now hung above the fireplace, the bullet still embedded. She said, "If it were not for that piece of gold you wouldn't be here. You never did tell me all about that Indian village."

For an instant the room filled with light for DiPaolo. He found himself back in the humid jungle, gazing at an ancient pyramid, surrounded with teaming life. He desired to return. Then the moment passed. The unlighted living room fell silent. He said to Benita, "Maybe some day I will tell you."

They were finally married at San Francisco City Hall. Then they took ship to spend a month in the Hawaiians. About eight months after the shooting, DiPaolo found he had one more errand. It was nothing required of him, but he felt he must do it. He went to visit Kwanyin Luk at the hospital. The chief of staff himself escorted DiPaolo. They were accompanied by a muscular orderly equipped with a straight jacket, just in case.

The Chief said, "You understand this is the criminally insane section of our hospital. Other areas are not so grim. If you like, I can show you around later."

"I would like that, Doctor." DiPaolo could see there was nothing lying around loose in this wing. The windows were all barred. Nothing that could be used as a weapon.

"I don't think this man will last much longer," the Chief said. "That wound to his knee developed gangrene. We had to amputate, and he has never quite recovered. He has had two heart attacks."

DiPaolo nodded. He knew that already. It was the main reason he had decided to come now. The Chief asked, "I have not followed the case closely. Didn't he have accomplices?"

"Oh, yes. The main one was a fellow calling himself O'Shea. He wasn't charged with the shooting, but he's in Leavenworth. Mail fraud, grand theft. There were a few others involved, Kwanyin's agents. Most of them were let go, it being too hard to prove anything. Oh, and there was a woman, a Mrs. Jones. She was charged but let off."

"Here is Mr. Kwanyin's cell. Do you want to be alone with him?"

He shrugged. "Not really. I'm only here to say hello. I'll give him a chance to talk if he wants to."

Kwanyin sat in a chair that was bolted to the floor. A blanket covered him. Apparently he had been reading a book, which had fallen on the floor. He woke up when the door opened. He blinked. "Dinner already? Oh, it's you. DiPaolo. Why are you still alive?"

"Why is any of us?"

Kwanyin threw off the blanket. "Your bitch of a woman did this. They tried to give me a wooden leg but it didn't work."

"I'm sorry, Luk. You should have gone back to Hong Kong."

"You should go to Hell." Then, oddly, he gave a twisted smile. DiPaolo was shocked at how the man's face had aged. Kwanyin said, "But it was some fun while it lasted, wasn't it?"

"Is there anything you need?"

"What more could I need? A bed, food, all the books I can read. Is there anything *you* require? Would you like to borrow money?"

Their conversation lasted a few more minutes, but DiPaolo realized there was nothing really to discuss. He had come to see his old enemy. He had seen him. When the time was right, he left the cell. Kwanyin said nothing, but raised a hand in salute.

The Chief took DiPaolo on a tour of the rest of the institution. It covered several acres, with much to see. Thinking about his visit,

DiPaolo stopped the Chief. He said, "What did Kwanyin mean about lending me money? Does he have some?"

The Chief turned to look at him with some surprise. "You have not been reading all the papers, then. The hospital here has a legal responsibility to manage the patient's property, including his bank accounts. You mentioned that some of Kwanyin's agents are still out there. Many of his victims still refuse to believe they are victimized. They still believe the di Paolo estate is real, and they will profit from their investments. Some of them even refuse to believe that 'Pascual' is Kwanyin, and that he is in an institution. They are still sending him money."

Now DiPaolo stared. He said, "How much?"

"Oh. I'm not directly involved with that problem. I last saw the book about a month ago. That's just the receipts that have come in since he was committed. I believe it now stands at about one and a half million dollars."

<<<<>>>>

Milton Keynes UK
Ingram Content Group UK Ltd.
UKHW010421131223
434231UK00001B/81